S0-BAX-407

DONE DEAL

Two wheels on the grass, the blue four-door was nudged against the fence, passably nondescript except for the hood ornament.

Twice I looked at it. There was a loose sprawl of seersucker suit, bent knees, white socks, big shoes, bony wrists, long arms spread wide to hug the sky. Wire across the chest and around the wrists, a metal collar around the neck that seemed attached to a chain wound through the side windows.

Roxbury Parker's bent knee straightened as his heel slipped off the hood. His collapsing leg thumped the metal.

The sound that followed was much louder. A white flash enveloped the car . . .

Most Pocket Books are available at special quantity discounts for bulk purchases for sales promotions, premiums or fund raising. Special books or book excerpts can also be created to fit specific needs.

For details write the office of the Vice President of Special Markets, Pocket Books, 1230 Avenue of the Americas, New York, New York 10020.

BROKERED DEATH

A DONALD McCARRY MYSTERY

JOHN C. BOLAND

POCKET BOOKS

New York   London   Toronto   Sydney   Tokyo   Singapore

This book is a work of fiction. Names, characters, places and
incidents are either products of the author's imagination or are
used fictitiously. Any resemblance to actual events or locales or
persons, living or dead, is entirely coincidental.

An *Original* Publication of POCKET BOOKS

POCKET BOOKS, a division of Simon & Schuster Inc.
1230 Avenue of the Americas, New York, NY 10020

Copyright © 1991 by John C. Boland

All rights reserved, including the right to reproduce
this book or portions thereof in any form whatsoever.
For information address Pocket Books, 1230 Avenue
of the Americas, New York, NY 10020

ISBN: 0-671-74097-0

First Pocket Books printing January 1992

10 9 8 7 6 5 4 3 2 1

POCKET and colophon are registered trademarks of
Simon & Schuster Inc.

Cover art by John Nickle

Printed in the U.S.A.

For John Rees

1

THE MARKET WAS HAVING A ROUGH AFTERNOON. YOU CAN
tell by the mutter of the ticker. On a good day, as the
big trades come over, it purrs. On a bad one the
machine coughs out the numbers in staccato burps, as
if all of corporate America has indigestion. Today was
one of those. I had gone out to lunch making money
on my favorite gimmicky stock and came back to find
that I was in the hole by four hundred dollars.
Four-eighty if I counted lunch at the Canterbury
Room for a client who wasn't worth it.

I walked through the crowd in the lobby, watching
the price board. The marching red numbers reported
that the major stock indices had fallen sharply in the
last two hours. The world was a few billion dollars
poorer, and most of its inhabitants didn't know or

care. Customers of the firm jostled against me, along with sightseers who had wandered in from the street. Both groups made noises about which way the market was bound to jump in the next few minutes. It had sunk forty points in less than an hour, so there was a lot of betting on a rally. The market ignored the bettors and dropped four more points.

I elbowed my way forward, picking out the symbols of stocks that I owned or had bought for clients. A couple seemed to be holding on, but most were giving away eighths and quarters. It suddenly felt like a long afternoon ahead. Customers would be unhappy, or angry, or scared. Weak markets turned people sentimental about money they used to have and surly toward the brokers they blamed for losing it. The office manager would be grumbling because brokers' sales productivity was down.

Nothing for it, I thought. Holding hands went with the job, even if you weren't good at it.

As I turned toward the elevator, Magee & Temple's chairman made his afternoon appearance in the lobby. He did it without fuss and bother, just an elegant older gentleman come around to watch the march of prices with the commoners. The lobby was designed for such nineteenth-century gestures. A gilt-trimmed balcony at the east end supported an electronic price board beneath the railing. Nearby on the lobby floor, out of the way of the elevator traffic, a marble table held a dozen telephones that connected to the trading desk. It was assumed that anyone who watched the changing prices long enough would be seized by an urge to buy or sell something.

The afternoon visits were a tradition Thornton Wacker had inherited along with his title as chairman four years ago. For three decades his father had come down to mingle with the public every day, except when traveling for his health. So Gilman-Groton-Yale-Oxford Thorny showed up most days, resplen-

2

dent in silver-streaked black hair and Savile Row navy, getting into his late sixties, proud he could dip a toe into the sea of humanity without shuddering.

I walked on without seeing whether anyone who recognized him dared approach.

Most of the business that the firm's populism drummed up didn't pay its way. On a typical account, small commissions barely covered the bookkeeping costs. And seeming too democratic could hurt a firm that relied mainly on the carriage trade. The craggy-browed old boys and little ladies who summered on Block Island expected brokers to be social climbers, straining to press their lips to the backside just overhead while standing on the fingers of the loser a rung below. The little ladies knew that this competition had made America a moral beacon. Thorny Wacker understood all that. He understood that one admired clients' intelligence, moral character, and cultural tastes in direct proportion to the mailing weight of their bank statements. He understood that it was useless to give a wage earner the time of day. Yet foremost he understood that democracy was a tradition at Magee & Temple, and old money revered even asinine traditions.

I pushed my way onto the elevator.

Meg Sorkin, the secretary for the four brokers whose offices surrounded her workstation, gave me a wide smile. "Hi, Donald. Mr. Oberfeld was looking for you."

Max Oberfeld was the office manager. Oberfuehrer to the brokers on the eighteenth floor. Mad Max to everyone who knew him. I smiled back and asked, "Did he say what for?"

"No, he didn't. And Miss Kimball called." She accented the last syllable, so the name sounded like a Chinese sporting event. Stacy Kimball's father probably owned a kick-boxing team or two somewhere in the corporate tree.

3

"Anybody else?"

She ignored the spike on which she impaled phone messages, coffee-and-Danish receipts, and most of Max's directives. "No one else. It looks like you'll be left alone this afternoon."

"You invoke the kindest fates," I said. I went into my office, hung up my jacket, and checked the quote machine. My retailing stock, Presto-Wok International, had fallen seventy-five cents a share from where it had started the day. Presto-Wok manufactured small appliances in the Far East, imported them to a base in Connecticut, and sold them by mail order. The company's growth had been spectacular, because the market for cheap appliances was apparently bottomless. Presto-Wok could sell an Appalachian housewife a stir-fry pan one week for twenty dollars, then come back two weeks later and get ten dollars for an adapter that turned the pan into a waffle iron. It looked like a stock that could go straight to the moon.

With the market tumbling, my imagination entertained less celestial possibilities. Suppose Presto-Wok's sales growth had been trumped up. Suppose unsold fry pans were stacked to the ceiling in a South Norwalk warehouse. Suppose the chief financial officer and the head auditor had eloped to an extradition-free zone. Tomorrow the company would apologetically file for bankruptcy protection, and the stock would drop from twenty-one dollars a share to half a buck.

I held a thousand shares that I had bought last night on margin. I called downstairs to Cheryl on the trading desk. "Dump that thousand Presto-Wok at twenty and three-quarters or better." That happened to be the current price.

I set the receiver down, went out to Meg's domain, and poured a cup of coffee. None of my colleagues had shown himself for a while. The door to the east corner office was closed as usual. Art Bradshaw had been with Magee & Temple longer than any of us and socialized the least. Idle chatter took time away from selling limited partnerships with commissions as high as twelve percent. Art boasted that he could close any client on any product in less than five minutes. He had three kids in private schools to prove it.

On most days I would have run into the suite's two other occupants a half-dozen times by now. I asked Meg, "Are Timmy and Isaiah in?"

"Mr. Upham's wife is ill, and Isaiah is downstairs meeting with Mr. Oberfeld."

My office antennae were beginning to twitch. Art and Timmy had hired Meg and briefed her so that she almost knew a stock from a bond. The arrangement made her more our person than a Max Oberfeld operative. I said, "Any idea why they're meeting?"

"Unh-unh. Want me to ask?"

"No, that's okay." I went back into my office. I had no intention of responding to Max's message. When Isaiah Stern came back, I could sound him out. The last event that had required lots of parleying with Max had been Magee & Temple's new policy reducing the percentage of commissions that brokers could keep.

Cheryl called back and said we had gotten twenty-one for the stock, better than I had hoped. Glancing at the screen, I saw it had crept back up to twenty-one and an eighth.

Never apologize for being a coward, my father counseled. It was about all his wisdom.

I picked the receiver up again in mid-ring. A nasal baritone drawled at me, insistently recognizable. "Donald, this is Patrick Squires," he said, except that it didn't sound that way. Off Patrick's tongue, single syllables grew multiple personalities. Names came out Don-*ald, Pa*-trick, *Squi*-res. He was an institutional stock salesman who had left Magee & Temple a year ago for one of our competitors. He said, "Do we still have our date for this evening?"

"Our date?"

"The Port-*fo*-lio Club," he prodded warmly. "It promises to be a *mem*-orable evening. You must remember? Gus-*tav* Raab?"

Raab was a European money manager who had set up shop in New York. Patrick and I had been comparing stock ideas a couple of weeks ago when he mentioned that Raab was to speak at the Portfolio Club. He volunteered to get me admitted.

The prospect of meeting a substantial money manager made me interested. He might have extra brokerage commissions to sprinkle around.

The downside of the deal was attending with Patrick and listening to his tales of woe, which focused on the cruelty of aging. He was in his early forties, a nightly devotee of a racquetball club or boxing gymnasium.

"It's good of you to remind me," I said.

"Sevenish, let's say, at the bar? We can compare heartbreaks."

"See you then," I said, deciding to arrive as the bar cleared for dinner at eight.

2

LUCIUS ASTENBERG HAD FOUNDED THE PORTFOLIO CLUB after being barred from the dining room of the New York Stock Exchange. His offense, which occurred in 1937, was rumored to have been tossing a shrimp cocktail into the face of a floor broker. The broker happened to be a governor of the exchange. Sitting on buy orders, he had blocked young Lucius from getting the jump on a group of traders who were planning to drive up the price of Radio Corporation's stock. The promoters, to whom the floor broker was loyal, wanted a surge of other buyers after they had their shares, not before.

Membership in the Portfolio Club was open to anyone in the financial district except floor brokers. In practice Lucius Astenberg blackballed everyone against whom he had a grudge. That was a list long enough to fill the charters of several rival clubs.

Meetings were informal, a two-hour cash bar at the same Wall Street restaurant for twenty years, then dinner and a speech in the next room. The food was always good. Lucius Astenberg was always present, a wizened white-faced wart in a wheelchair, to make certain that none of his old enemies slipped past the door. Most of them would have had grave moss on their neckties.

Patrick Squires was over by the raw bar, pitching a fund manager on the virtues of all the undiscovered billion-dollar companies that Patrick alone understood. Topic for tonight: "Why Is Digital Equipment a Great Company?" I could recite Patrick's preamble without eavesdropping. "You would sup-*pose* there's nothing new to be said about Digital Equipment, wouldn't you? But what most analysts don't understand . . ." He was totally sincere. Whatever old war-horse he mounted, however many man-hours Wall Street spent adding up the company's outlays for paper clips and dividing by its sales momentum, Patrick always claimed to have a unique insight. "What nobody understands about IBM . . ." "What the Street doesn't recognize about American Telephone . . ." And sometimes, derisively, "What the group-think crowd can't con-*cept*-ualize about *Dis*-ney . . ."

The essay that followed was invariably based on an

idea that had been talked about on the Street for weeks.

I ducked into the dining room, looking for Gustav Raab. A round, goateed form was the center of a small crowd, not besieged, because nobody would admit to holding anyone else in awe, but casually surrounded by people who leaned left or right as though they really should be rushing somewhere else.

Nuzzling a drink, I edged close enough to catch a couple of minor names spilling from the purple lips. "Oh, Michel ees an intuitive investor—grasps efferyzing I say to him—and I think thees proves that eet ees all in the genes, all in gentle, aristocratic blood. That is why the reech are reech." Not to mention, I supposed, why the super-reech were super-reech.

From what I'd heard it wasn't clear whether Raab had signed up many American clients since opening an office in New York. If his European base was big enough, he might have all the business he wanted and could be scouting the States for places to invest. The hangers-on chuckled at his insight—and hadn't they always wondered why they weren't rich?—and angled for seats at his table. As they moved away, his whole odd shape was visible. The head, with its pink cheeks, round forehead, and slicked black hair, was disproportionately tiny. Credit the genes, which bred out a money manager's least necessary parts. If you started with a bowling pin—one of the squat ones, a duckpin—and painted on it a goatee and a double-breasted suit, with red splashes for a bow tie and a carnation, the result would look a lot like Gustav Raab. When he shuffled around the table, he wobbled like a pin that had survived a near miss.

A hand landed on my shoulder, too high to be Lucius Astenberg coming to throw me out. Patrick Squires gave me a stern frown, instantly followed by a melting smile. "Terribly rude of you, Don-*ald.*"

Being late, he meant.

He was neatly turned out, butterscotch flannels, powder-blue shirt, pink foulard tie, diamond-studded tie bar, and a gold Rolex that he managed to display by folding his arms and letting the left wrist drape on the outside. He looked down from his gangly six-three, all nose and forehead and cheekbones, with pale hazel eyes that flickered self-consciously away from contact.

"If I had come any later," I said, "I wouldn't have heard about the reech and why they're wreetched."

There was another man with Patrick, a tweedy pipe smoker named Terrence Lippert who hung out at financial district bars. He had shaggy ginger hair, a narrow bony face, and a frozen skeptical smirk. He wrote a column for a glossy magazine, *Investor's Week*.

"Are you interested in Gustav Raab?" I asked Lippert.

"Thinking of a profile. He's cosmopolitan enough to impress our readers." Lippert's pipe stem wiggled as he got his words out past the obstruction. "I imagine half his staff have titles of some kind."

"Half of Europe has titles of some kind," Patrick countered.

Lippert shrugged, but the pipe tilted up in defiance, like a flag over a besieged fortress. He tried to stick his chin out at the same time. It was a dangerous combination. I waited for the pipe bowl to empty onto his nose.

"Have you interviewed Raab yet?" I asked.

"No. His office runs interference. I'm surprised that he turned out for tonight. This much exposure is rare for Gustav Raab. Old Lucius tells me they've known each other for years. So I guess it comes under the heading of indulging a friend."

"I've met him," Patrick volunteered. "He deals

with his own little circle of brokers. He doesn't want to hear anyone else's ideas."

Most of the Portfolio Club members who had shown up were male. The presentable woman had been cornered, and the other one appeared to chew tobacco. I sat with Patrick and the writer. A portfolio manager from Citibank joined us, drinking his way through dinner and mumbling about MagnaRam Computer Corporation, which apparently had failed to open for business this morning. The kitchen rolled out trolleys of something wrapped in pastry. Lucius Astenberg took his nourishment intravenously. Before dessert or coffee had showed, Lucius craned forward at the head table, clanging a spoon on a glass.

"It's my pleasure—my pleasure—gentlemen, if you'll shut up, to introduce the head magician at Raab Capital Limited. If you don't know who Gus Raab is, you shouldn't be here. So this is a short introduction, befitting an old man's lungs. I'll turn it right over to our guest. Gus?"

Raab beamed above his goatee and spent ten minutes uttering banalities about the benefits of internationalizing portfolios. The topic was fascinating only to people obsessed with the stock market. Even to my normally receptive ear, Raab's observations were as stale as Patrick Squires's stock tips. He had a professorial habit of stressing every point with a finger jabbing the air. Fewer jabs could have explained quantum theory.

The louder and faster he spoke, the thicker the accent grew. He said, *"For efferay reezk een beink an eenternazzional eenvestor . . ."* and I listened hard and translated, "For every risk in being an international investor . . ." Then I missed the next line, which presumably cited some offsetting benefit. Gradually my ear filtered out most of the *eez*s and *zee*s except when he worked himself toward a crescendo.

"As professional investors, we would never—never!—limit ourselves to investing only in companies in a certain city or state. And I suggest that our view of the investment world not be blinded—blinded!—by archaic *national* boundaries."

Wendell Willkie would have approved.

He got polite applause, and I wondered in disappointment if the guy was really such a soft noodle.

Patrick Squires whispered intently, "Something to think about, hmm, Don-*ald?*"

"A revelation," I agreed.

The Citibank manager piped up. "What I wonder is, if you're too stupid to make money in the U.S., why should you do better going international? Someone answer me that."

Terrence Lippert tucked his pen into the spirals of his notebook. "It works because you escape the information overload. You're too close to U.S. companies. You may actually know what's going on in them."

The banker shook his head. "Usually I don't. Take MagnaRam Computer. A week ago the treasurer said they were doing okay. Today the phone doesn't answer."

"That's just my point," Lippert insisted. "If the company were in Milan or Stockholm, you'd never have heard they were doing okay."

Balancing my coffee, I squeezed between tables and blocked Lucius Astenberg's wheelchair. "Splendid as usual, Mr. Astenberg."

Bleary pink eyes looked up and puzzled. His voice was a cranky hinge. "I am happy to hear that you enjoyed it, Mr.—" A scowl. A hairless wrinkled brow lifted. "Are you a member?"

"A guest of Mr. Squires. My name is Donald McCarry. I'm with Magee & Temple."

"Did Mr. Squires pay for your meal?"

"I'm certain he did."

11

"In that event, it is a pleasure to have you here, Mr. uhmpf, agh, ha, a pleasure. Now if you will kindly get the hell out of my Cadillac's way."

"Yes sir."

I turned my back and excused myself once or twice for elbows before I reached Gustav Raab. The group surrounding him was thin but determined. A couple of smaller money managers were curious about a man who handled a rumored half-billion upper-class dollars. Several brokers, like me, held a quaint hope of snaring some of his commissions.

I shouldered past the tobacco-chewing woman, who headed a research boutique on Water Street. My opening line was down pat. When the round, bearded face turned my way, I rolled it out. "You have put a lot of my own thinking into words, Mr. Raab. Our colleagues understand spreading a portfolio's risk out among different industries. But the wisdom of spreading out risk among countries is not widely accepted."

It had been common practice for ten years. But he accepted the role of trailblazer with a smug nod. "It will be, young man."

"Yes, results speak eloquently, don't they? By the way, I'm Donald McCarry. I handle business for a few clients who are willing to look abroad."

Were Trenton and Milwaukee abroad?

"So nice to meet you, Mr. McCarry. It is a pity that we have not connected before. Do particular countries seem attractive to you just now?" When he wasn't trying to project, his voice was syrupy, like the purr Charlie Boyer used on Hedy Lamarr. It was easier to follow. He tilted forward, rocked back, righting himself with a faint tremor.

Particular countries? Between university semesters and jobs, I had visited Mexico, England, and France. I had a vague notion that Hong Kong and Japan had stock markets. Everybody talked about the Japanese stock market. When I thumbed *Investor's Week*, I never glanced at the international pages. Too many awkward foreign names.

I handed Raab my business card, the one that said Senior Vice President, an exaggeration that Magee & Temple had never noticed. "Perhaps we could compare notes at our leisure."

"I do not have much leisure," Raab said, with pride and regret. He extended a tiny blue card bearing enough ornate engraving to include his ancestry. "But like minds should, heh, cross-pollinate."

He was also a brilliant botanist.

3

I SET OUT TO HOOK GUSTAV RAAB.

Half a billion pedigreed bucks, if that was what he managed for his elegants, could produce five million a year in broker commissions if the broker did his job. Mainly the job was sitting in a chair and dreaming up ideas that would cause the client to buy and sell stocks. The part of the account that was earmarked for aggressive trading could be turned over like a flapjack three or four times a year, the rest at least once.

Not that I would get all of Raab's business. But one-tenth of the pool would finance a Catskills cottage and put me on Thorny Wacker's dinner list.

So I ripped the international columns from office copies of *Investor's Week* and sent a messenger around town collecting annual reports from mutual funds that bought foreign stocks. I tried phoning Bill Hinsdale, a college classmate who worked in the Paris office of Merrill Lynch, but he was taking a few days' holiday. Even without Bill's input, three days of crash reading gave me a creditable line of double-talk.

I hid my plans from Timmy Upham, Art Bradshaw, and Isaiah Stern. Dropped just enough hints to Mad Max that he left me alone. Phoned Raab Capital's office twice without getting through. Boasted extravagantly to Stacy Kimball that Gustav Raab was in the bag. She was skeptical. "You can't become an expert on international stock markets in three days, sweetheart."

"Experts have been made in less time."

We had driven up the Connecticut coast and rented a day sailer for an idle Sunday. She dragged a hand in the water. "But you can't fool a real expert."

"I'm not trying to fool him. I've done my research. I even called Paris."

"Your interest is all of three days old. Do you plan to tell him that?"

"It's not relevant."

"You're trying to fool him," she said conclusively. She could be difficult. She had no vanity that needed powdering. She had no incentive to cooperate when somebody wanted to fool her.

I was counting on Raab being all vanity.

"All right," she said, "let's assume you bamboozle Raab. Will that make you a wiser, better person?" Her left eye, the only one I could see, was ready for mischief.

"It will make me more prosperous. By your family's standards, that will make me a wiser, better, nobler, and gentler person. But do I want to be wiser, better, and so on? Would I be as much fun if I were better?"

She put her face down and laughed. "Who says you're fun?"

"Your sister Betsy."

"Come on! She's only met you twice. She thinks you're old."

"But fun." I rolled over and stared into the water. It lay a few inches from my face, slapping on the hull. The tiny sail was luffing on the warm air as we wallowed in slow, backward circles. Neither of us had bothered to pull the sheet tight in twenty minutes. Instead we bickered about Gustav Raab and played two-sided Botticelli, which didn't work. Stacy chose an Italian painter only she had heard of. I retaliated with Jesse Livermore, one of the great stock speculators of the twenties, but she guessed him after a dozen questions.

"I know your points of reference," she said.

They weren't elusive. I liked the stock market and the Mets and could take or leave most everything else. Calvin Coolidge and Jesse Livermore met my vague notion of admirable characters, though it troubled me a little that Livermore, having lost his final million, had sipped a drink at the Sherry-Netherland one afternoon before dropping into the gents' to put a bullet through his head.

Then again, I had never made or lost a million—let alone a million when it was serious money. Today the income from one piddling million wouldn't support anyone in lavish comfort. If you got up to a couple of dozen million, life could be interesting. It still wasn't big-time money, but one could pass. It would support a respectable yacht on the French Riviera (as long as the yacht was chartered by the month), riding low under the weight of foie gras, fresh South American shrimp, cases of Pomerol and sunscreen, and radio telephones, telex, fax, and quote terminals for mucking around in the world's stock markets. You could call a broker at midnight and scream, "Buy London—sell short New York!" Then dinner in Monte Carlo, with a turn at *chemin de fer*. The vision of a million-aire's life shimmered like a ghost in a distant summer haze.

When the money piled up higher than desk level, a fellow like Gustav Raab would be called in, handed a few million with instructions to feed and water it, make it grow thirty percent without taking big risks.

"Do you want to go back to shore?" Stacy asked.

"Sure. Do you think we could rent the couch in the boathouse for a half hour?"

"Are you breathing heavily?" She leaned forward to see. "You must have been daydreaming about money."

As I said, impossible to fool.

We tightened the sail and caught an edge of slow air that pulled us toward the merrymakers on the beach and campground. It was a warm afternoon, and the breeze on the Sound was like an asthmatic's last gasp. They were closing up shop at the boat-rental emporium. A snub-nosed blond kid sneered at my sunburn. "We've got pedal boats, you know."

"McCarry demands a challenge," Stacy said.

McCarry got his deposit back minus twenty dollars and followed his smart-alecky lady friend up the path to a band shell crowded with little wrought-iron tables. We got beers and found we didn't have much to talk about. Stacy didn't ask what Donald thought of the afternoon or of the world political order. Donald didn't ask if the beer was cold. The silence could mean either that we were content or that boredom was settling in. If she was bored, I didn't expect to know about it until after the summer's social doldrums. A practical girl didn't throw out old jackets and skirts when prospects were dim for finding something new.

"Do you want to drive back to town tonight?" I asked.

"What about you?"

16

"Well, on the one hand, we could have dinner at Reggie's. That's a plus. On the other, it would deprive your father of another chance at me. Also a plus. Does he deserve more than one shot per weekend?"

"Charlie Kimball deserves whatever he wants," she said of her father. Then added, "He's been perfectly civil to you."

He was a solemn little man whom I secretly liked while knowing the sentiment wasn't returned. Months ago I had tried to sign up Charlie Kimball as an account. Getting the brokerage commissions was only part of my goal. Mr. Charlie had good contacts that would be useful. He pretended to consider the idea. "Don't you think it would be awkward?" he asked.

"How so?"

"You would expect to keep the account after Stacy gets tired of you. And you wouldn't, of course." He smiled at my baleful look. "I know my daughter, and you're not her idea of husband material. She intends to be very careful on that point."

He strolled out of the library and left me to admire the family trophies staring glassy-eyed from the wall. All were legal game, bushwhacked fair and square. There would be a separate room somewhere for the carcasses of politicians and bankers who had gotten in the family fortune's way.

But old Charlie was right. Money didn't stay together for generations if you dissipated it on sons-in-law who brought in no dowry but had a sleeveful of investment ideas. He reminded me of a joke going around Magee & Temple's office about how many stockbrokers it took to wreck a fortune. The answer went, "Just one; stockbrokers know their stuff."

Timmy Upham had told me that one. He had been impressed by the name Kimball. "You've been wiggling toe-to-toe with an heir to the Lost Dutchman Mine. Charlie Kimball—that's her old man, isn't it?—is from the Tracer Minerals clan. His grandfather, I think it was, bought up a lot of Dakota mining claims when the Indians were on a rampage. Who would you bet incited the Indians?" He patted my arm, bestowing approval. "You really are a fortune hunter, buddy."

4

WE DROVE BACK TO TOWN, HAD DINNER AT REGGIE'S, AND spent the night at my SoHo loft. On Monday morning, Stacy headed off for her job at the Hammer Gallery and I set out to recoup last week's losses.

No mail-order operations. But a small hospital supply company called Diagnostic Research seemed to be acting strong. I bought a little and scalped a half-point by quitting time. After costs, I was about three hundred dollars better off than when I walked in.

Timmy Upham showed up at my office, his thumbs behind his suspenders, lower lip stuck out, brow pinched—wasting all that thoughtfulness on me. It was the look he put on for clients before spilling The Story on whatever stock he wanted them to buy. Timmy had taken a few hours of college philosophy, and he offered treatises on his companies—big pictures, how the changing shape of young urban gay professional life would remake the market for light wines. Next breath: he knew a couple of companies that were staking out the market ahead of everyone

18

else. He had studied history as well and fitted the latest fad into a perspective of centuries-long social evolution if his customers sat still for it. He had a long boyish face and an utterly cynical smile that the clients never glimpsed.

"Did you see Presto-Wok on the tape?" he said, referring to the news wire. A warning flicker of a smile escaped like a bird breaking cover.

I pretended indifference. "Why should I care about Presto-Wok?"

Timmy shrugged. "They're raising the dividend. The stock is up three points. If only we had bought a few days ago."

I stared him straight in the eye and didn't answer.

Timmy put his hands in his pockets. "The rise in the price poses a dilemma for me, a moral dilemma."

"The peskiest kind," I said.

"It just happened that I threw in an order to buy five hundred Presto-Wok shares this morning. Pure luck. I hadn't got a whisper that anything was up. Just damned good luck." He lifted his chin and smiled at a high corner.

"You've got a knack for being smug," I said. "But it was a nice trade, so congratulations."

He grinned. "I haven't told you about the dilemma. The trade wasn't meant to be for me. You know that little pension account I've got from Waxter Pharmaceuticals? The Presto-Wok was supposed to be for them. I put the order in, but something told me not to be in a hurry about writing a ticket assigning it to Waxter. Then right away the stock went up, and I just put off doing it. Here by blind luck I'd made fifteen hundred bucks for them. And my cut would be a hundred bucks commission. Kind of disproportionate, considering that the luck had been mine."

"On the other hand," I said, "you get the commissions even when the client loses money."

"But the client gets his shot at a profit," Timmy said without, as far as I could tell, a stammer or a hiccup.

"Okay, what's the end of this story?"

"When Cheryl called back a few minutes ago, demanding a name for the trade, I took it for myself."

"You're a cad," I said.

He bowed. "Pleased to meet you. I'll buy something for Waxter tomorrow. Tonight I'm taking Miss Sorkin to dinner."

"Does she know about your moral lapse?"

"I'm hoping to arrange another one this very evening."

"You know Cheryl squeals to Mad Max."

He paused in the doorway. Behind the protruding suspenders I could see Miss Sorkin closing up her desk. Timmy followed my glance, the pride of possession already budding. He said, "Max won't kick. Nobody but me knows the trade wasn't for my account in the first place. You can't tell me you've never done the same thing?"

"You know better. But I don't let those trades go through Cheryl. Nobody else on the trading desk gives a damn. Cheryl probably keeps a diary."

He shrugged and left. Even if Cheryl kept a history of his sins, Magee & Temple would turn a blind eye to anything that didn't threaten to become public knowledge. Timmy was playing by the house rules. When our senior partners came across a sweet morsel, it went into their own accounts before brokers and clients got pieces. There were never enough sweet morsels to go around.

I killed an hour by calling a few clients. Dangling bits of news or rumor scrounged from the Dow Jones wire, I hooked a couple of orders for tomorrow's opening bell. My business was beginning to remind me of selling bikinis to Eskimo squaws. You couldn't care if they didn't fit—less that they weren't needed

—because the job was to close the sale and earn the commission.

That aspect of the business was beginning to taste bad. If my perception shifted just a little, Timmy Upham would look less like an endearingly cynical preppy and more like a pickpocket. My perception of Donald McCarry was shaky too.

Wavering was a vision of the bright young fellow destined for great things. Swimming into sight was a middle-aged huckster with a worn line of empty patter.

It was close to five o'clock, so I called the gallery and asked for Stacy. I said, "We could have dinner uptown."

"Bad timing. I'm flogging a Neiman to a blind matron. Let me call you back." She hung up.

I hung up, and the phone rang.

A saucy British tart's voice said, "Mr. Donald McCarry? This is Herr Gustav Raab's office calling. Would you hold please?"

He came on right away. "Would you have dinner with me this evening, Mr. McCarry? At my town house, please?"

I almost offered to bring Chinese carryout. Then I adopted a matter-of-fact tone that hinted that this was short notice but I would do anything for a client. It probably just sounded eager. "Why, yes, I'd be glad to."

"Seven o'clock, if it is convenient?"

"Fine, I'm looking forward—"

"I will expect you." He hung up.

Digging out his business card, I found an address on East Seventy-second Street that must be near Central Park. It was a nice neighborhood full of granite-faced mansions that had been built for Guggenheims and Pulitzers. A city ordinance required that stockbrokers who visited the neighborhood had to be kept on leashes so they wouldn't wrap themselves around a gentleman's leg.

I glanced at the clock, added six or seven hours, and phoned Bill Hinsdale in Paris. He lived in an old part of the Right Bank that he complained had been taken over by gay bars. When the government nationalized the last bank and bakery, Bill said, there would still be laissez-faire in gay bars.

A Mozart piece was piping along in the background of his apartment, and voices chattered. Even on a Monday evening some cities put a good party ahead of life's trivial chores. "I thought you were coming over this summer," he said.

"First I've got to pull in a client who thinks I know something about foreign markets."

"That should be a snap. Your clients think you know something about the U.S. market."

"This fellow is less easily deceived. He's in a position to know things himself. I need a fact, something he can bite on, check out and confirm, and make money on. Is anybody getting taken over that you know about?"

Bill chuckled. "Would you take over a company in France? The whole idea is to sneak your wealth out to the U.S. or Switzerland—though you can't trust the Swiss anymore—anyway, get it out before the Bolshies take over." He was silent, and I could catch a phrase or two from his friends. Finally Bill said, "Let me pick up the bedroom line."

In a moment he was back. "This isn't information known around the firm, but Marie and I have been buying. Her brother Benjy represents ECB, that's Electronics Corporation of Belgium, on some local business, and Benjy heard something. They're laying a new transatlantic phone cable next year, you know, the first since the seventies. ECB will get a major contract."

"How can you be sure?"

"It's being announced on Thursday."

"How big is major?"

"Their share is about forty million dollars over eighteen months. It should add ten points to the stock right away, a quick thirty percent. Benjy has borrowed money from everyone he knows to buy the shares. When he tried borrowing from Marie, I wrung the story out of him."

"Tell me more about ECB."

As he rattled off details, I took notes. As to why ECB was a shoo-in for the work, Bill grew vague. Basically, their technology could compress more conversations onto a single line than anyone else's could, by exploiting the pauses between words and syllables.

After Bill went back to his party, I dug through the columns I had clipped from *Investor's Week* and found a couple of references to ECB. Nothing hinted at new business. But I memorized some authentic-sounding fragments, the better to snow Herr Raab.

5

THE BRIGHT EVENING LIGHT DID WONDERS FOR EAST Seventy-second Street. Facades were sepia and sidewalks were hammered copper. Trees had lain down as long shadows in the street, discouraging traffic from roaring down from the avenues. It was too quiet for the leaf shadows to dare rustle.

Raab had a secretary named Mullins with a blond

crew cut. I didn't think the tarty English accent belonged to him. Mullins was tall, healthy, and as Germanic as a tank. He wore a double-breasted navy suit like his master's but about eight sizes larger across the chest and two smaller in the hips. Raab was a duckpin, and Mullins was one of those cardboard Phillip Morris manikins, all upper torso dwindling to tiny toes. He didn't wear a bellman's box hat, which would have sissified the crew cut.

Mullins sat me in a drawing room lined with books up to the ceiling. Otherwise the place was pretty bare. A few Persian carpets, an iron-breasted fireplace, two Louis Quinze sofas, six or seven matching chairs with red satin upholstery and gilt legs, and a marquetry desk where a few odds and ends of the czar's Fabergé collection had been tossed in passing. Then a couple of occasional tables, the one at my hand bearing distress marks that testified it had been around when the Tories were losing Manhattan.

Mullins didn't say whether Herr Raab would be along in a minute. He walked out and closed the door. The room was supposed to entertain me. I guessed it would if I were an antiques fence toting a pocket calculator.

The room had two mullioned windows looking out onto a tiny side yard where a pair of hemlocks nudged the wall that held back the tackiness of the street. A ball of suet encased in wire hung from a low branch, and a squirrel had shinnied down and was trying to outsmart the wire.

It occurred to me that a guy who would do that to thwart a squirrel would have a pressure alarm under each Fabergé egg.

I dug out my crib sheet for a quick review of the little I knew about ECB. I barely got the thing out of sight as the door opened and Gustav Raab rolled in, palms hugging his hips in the pockets of a burgundy dinner jacket. Mullins came after and stood at attention.

"Delighted you could join me," Raab piped. "Bruno, Mr. McCarry has never tasted the perfect martini. Make him one."

Mullins went to a cabinet along the back wall that I had missed cataloging, an authentic-looking Roentgen, and fiddled among the hidden compartments with his steer-sized back blocking my view.

Raab inventoried his gold eggs, picked one off the desk, a gems-and-enamel affair the size of a tennis ball, and lifted the hinged upper half. He pouted at the hidden treasure, a tiny bird fashioned of gold wire with rubies for eyes. It had the breathtaking grace of life. "So beautiful, so absolutely beautiful," he announced. When he spoke calmly, the accent subsided. The zees and zisses were still there but started to sound normal. "Carl Fabergé made this for a Romanov princess in 1885, a time when the family's wealth was literally unimaginable. The wealth still exists, though in different hands." He flipped the lid down as if it belonged to a two-dollar snuffbox and set the egg back.

"Wealth has a way of dissipating," he observed. "The American vernacular has it exactly right—it is hard to hang on to a buck. Harder still with a thousand. All but impossible with grand amounts. Our appetites are often our undoing. If not gluttony, then external events."

The tilt of his head gave me a feeling there was more to the message than I heard: he seemed to be listening for an echo—Yes, our appetites or something. I didn't know what Raab's appetites were.

Before I could settle on a snappy response—a scornful sniff and "Some people have no respect for capital" seemed right—Raab's attention shifted as Mullins brought a tray of drinks.

"Bruno worked as a bartender at Baden-Baden many years ago," Raab said. "When I met him, he was back on his native soil as executive secretary to the president of a Swiss bank. His diversion into finance cost the world the services of a remarkable artist. But a bar attendant should enjoy human frailty, and Bruno has never had a sympathetic ear."

The martinis were nothing special, par for the Plaza, a cut below the Pierre. I hoped Mullins had excelled as a banker.

Raab made a production of enjoying his drink. Mullins's stony blue eyes watched with no trace of gratitude.

"Bruno, do you think we're ready to sit down?"

"I will inquire, Herr Raab." He tucked the tray under his arm and set off to break the cook's head.

Raab turned to me. "What area of the world particularly interests you right now?"

Only places with good restaurants and topless beaches. Those didn't overlap with the major financial centers, which seemed to have sprung up where people needed distractions during the rainy months. That wasn't an adequate answer for Raab. I tried something more in the spirit of our game. "We make money going where the action isn't—if that's clear."

"Exactly, exactly! One must avoid the crowd, buy cheap what the world has forgotten about. This is a splendid strategy."

Upping the ante, I said, "More a tactic than a strategy, really. The strategy is the search for investments that are selling for less than their real worth."

"No, young man, let me correct you. That which you speak of is a philosophy, the search for bona fide bargains. The philosophy informs the strategy, which is how you do it."

"Point taken," I said, giving an ingratiating nod. Shameless, Stacy's conscience hissed. Raab was tickled with himself. I said, "Some places where there is no crowd, there also are no bargains. A year or so ago I investigated the Nepalese market—"

"Now you are making a joke."

"It's quite small, a handful of textile companies. And the market in most shares is not active."

"But the companies—were they attractive?"

"It was difficult to know," I said, tapping out on my lore, "because the companies revealed little of their financial performances. The companies are controlled by tight-knit groups that don't like outsiders." The last was winging it. Because he didn't flinch, I switched to fabricating freestyle. "They're mostly concerned about raiders from New Delhi."

He drew back and chuckled. "You have created an odd image in my mind. The exchange—or bolsa or what it is called?—I envision in a yak pasture. Trading is conducted around smoky peat fires. A buyer bids four goat hides for a share of Nepal Carpet Mills. The idea is quite amusing. Now that you have had your joke, you must tell me if there is really a Nepalese securities market."

Mullins opened the door and said, "It's ready."

The dining room was cozy and understated, dimly lit by wall sconces on either side of a floor-to-ceiling gilt-trimmed mirror set between Doric demi-columns. The emperor wasn't joining us. His favorite muses fluttered around the chandelier. A tiny Korean woman brought in lobster bisque, and Raab fussed with opening a bottle of Pouilly-Fuissé. Mullins was off slaughtering the main course.

"Monsieur McCarry, how long have you been a customer's man?" Raab asked.

It was an archaic and genteel term for my job, customer's man. The trendier firms called their salesmen account executives. The more candid ones said salesmen.

27

"Seven years," I said.

"Magee & Temple enjoys a reputation in some circles. Are you happy there?"

I wondered if this was supposed to be a job interview. "Reasonably happy."

"Have you spent your career there?"

"The last four years of it. Before that, there was a year at Weil Brothers and a stint with Merrill."

His pale cheeks wiggled in distaste.

I hurried on. "It takes a while to find a firm that suits one's own investment style. Some people in this business have no style to speak of, no—"

"No philosophy?" He nodded his own answer. Grubbing dollars and yen sounded better as a philosophy. "It is the same in Europe. We have deal closers, merchandisers, supersalesmen, syndicators —everything, my dear boy, except professional, conscientious, scrupulous investors." No question which company he counted himself part of.

I matched his disapproval, ignoring Stacy's angry buzzing. "To a salesman, everything is just another product." If there were abstract justice ready and waiting in the world, the words would have choked me. Selling shopping center syndications and oil drilling programs had kept me alive for a couple of years when the stock market wouldn't twitch if you kicked it.

The gentlemanly broker who fitted his clients into stocks like a tailor measuring flannels was an anachronism who didn't do enough business to pay for his desk space. To earn your keep, you had to bring in ten-thousand-share trades from hyperactive pension funds.

Raab would know the business well enough to recognize that if I was still on the payroll at Magee & Temple, it was because I could sell hotel syndications with the next guy. So no point in grabbing his hand and crooning it was us nice girls versus the whores.

"I noticed you having a few words with Lucius Astenberg," Raab said. "Have you known him long?"

If it was a trap, it was crude. "We don't know one another at all," I said.

"Lucius is an astute investor," Raab said. "A great pretender as well. You would think him senile, but there has been no diminution of faculties. We met in Europe when he was putting together a partnership. That was many years ago. Lucius had the lawyers convinced that he could not remember his own name. Quite amusing. He would have them remind him of things. 'Oh, yes, oh, yes,' Lucius would sputter. Then he would ask in a tremulous voice if they had not meant to express their idea in such-and-such terms, which corrected an error in their formulation. He enjoyed himself enormously."

"Was the partnership successful?"

He didn't answer directly. "We both understand there are two measures of success in these things. Lucius was not particularly successful at raising capital; he was not well known. I believe the partnership began with less than two million dollars. By the other measure, it was a pleasant success. It came into the American market in the late sixties, when everything was going up. My friend was wise enough to leave the market with considerable profits in seventy-three. That avoided the rather nasty bear market."

"Not many people take the money and run," I said.

"Longevity helps. Lucius had been around long enough to learn from his errors."

The Korean woman brought in rack of lamb. On the side was a pearly puddle of marrow on a medallion of toast. Another bottle of wine—a rich Bordeaux—was poured and Raab popped his first glass down and said wetly, "The worst mistake in your business, my dear boy, is talkativeness. When I deal through a broker, I demand complete discretion. I cannot afford to have it known in financial circles that Raab is taking a position in Swiss chemicals. I am possibly buying only a small part of my total commitment through any single broker. If he is indiscreet, it will interfere with my other purchases. Many people will try to follow my lead, because they know Raab has business insights. They will drive up the price before I am finished. Discretion, my friend."

"That's the ground rule with most big clients," I said. Especially the megalomaniacs who believed the world followed their lead.

"A rule, yes—but too seldom observed."

He was exaggerating his importance. Most people didn't know his name. To most of those who did, Raab Capital was just another money-management firm with a European flavor. If I told Timmy Upham that I was buying Swiss chemicals for Raab, he would answer, "Everybody is buying something."

"What impresses me about you, young man, is that you have not been indiscreet this evening. You have not tried to impress me with the names of your other famous clients. You have not boasted of how you made Monsieur Corot's fortune or encouraged Baron Guy to invest in copper stocks."

"I've never dealt with either of them," I said.

"I appreciate your candor. Many of your colleagues claim some affiliation with great wealth."

"I like clients whose checks clear," I said. "Beyond that I don't check pedigrees."

"A broker of the people?" The derisive tone was close to the surface.

"Not a snob, let's say. Snobbishness is foolish in my business. Some of my best customers wear patched jackets and own a nut-and-bolt factory upstate. They know what makes a company run well, and what makes its stock cheap. I collect commissions off them and learn a lot."

"Well, I would like to bring a small amount of business to you—on an experimental basis—

provided I do not have to wear a patched jacket." He didn't ask if I was interested. From a pocket he produced a folded square of blue paper.

"Tomorrow morning, please begin buying these shares. You may use your discretion on the price, up to the ceilings I have listed. At the end of each day, you may call Bruno with a report on the transactions. Bruno will handle the formalities of establishing the account. It will be in the name of one of our subsidiaries, Rain Tree Capital."

There were a dozen names on the list. Mostly big, familiar American companies, good choices if the economy kept expanding.

"I think we should add one," I said. "Electronics Corporation of Belgium. My contacts look for very favorable developments."

"By all means. Buy up to twenty thousand shares." Raab was too short to give me a patronizing pat on the shoulder. His smile did the job.

6

IMRIE DE WOHL CAME AROUND A MONTH LATER.

He was boyish, wore three-hundred-dollar loafers made from his own lasts (he complained about his shoemaker), blue jeans, and an RAF jacket. His eyes were black and set close together, and he had either high eyebrows or a tiny forehead. His lips were wide and heavy and accustomed to pouting.

We kidded for a while about how I was a boffo broker, and he opened an account with an Israeli bank check for two million dollars. He said, "Buy what you want."

"Maybe some Swiss chemicals?"

"Do they have chemicals? Sure, go ahead, anything you want. Just double my stake."

"We might not do quite that well."

I had tried to guess how old he was, what his point of origin had been, and his role in life besides pretending to be an investor. Twenty-two, I supposed. Unguessable on the second: somewhere a nanny or au pair taught colloquial New York-London. On the third, who cared?

He uncrossed his legs and popped up. He'd already glanced around without finding anything interesting. He tried it once more. Lots of paper, and he knew what paper was, a quotation terminal which was generically just another computer, and no prints on the wall or amphoras on the shelves or whatever else would have interested him. "I'm off."

"Should I notify you of trades?"

"You do that? Each time?"

"I can. Or we can just send out monthly statements." Meg was typing up papers for a discretionary account. I wasn't sure I wanted him to hang around and sign them. Or just leave with or without the check.

"Well, monthly statements would be less labor-intensive. From my standpoint, I mean—you know, reading them."

Reading was a pain, I agreed.

"Okay, monthly," he said.

"Just in case something comes up, do you have an address in town?" He'd given me the name of a hotel, the Connaught, in London.

He patted his curly head. "Dunno, really. I'm just here overnight. Hopping up to Toronto tomorrow on U.S. Scare. You'd best send stuff to the Connaught. I'll be back there in August."

"Okay. If you want to check in before then, here's an eight hundred number."

He tucked my card into a shirt pocket. Too polite to pitch it right on the spot.

"You weren't very precise on who recommended Magee & Temple to you," I said.

"Just the grapevine."

I didn't smile. "This check—it won't be followed by large cash transactions?"

"Shouldn't think so, mate. Why lug cash around?"

"Some people like to. It can cause problems."

"Not my style. I'm just a passive investor. Or working on being one. I haven't got the lingo down yet."

He toodle-ooed.

I sat back and counted. If I flipped Imrie's two-million-dollar portfolio only four times a year, and collected one percent in commissions going and coming each time, that would create one hundred sixty thousand in raw commissions charges. Magee & Temple would let me keep forty percent of that, or sixty-four thousand. I wouldn't churn him that often. But I wouldn't turn that kind of account away just because Imrie de Wohl didn't know a common stock from a tulip bulb.

And I wouldn't let Imrie fool me all the way.

I went out and leaned against Meg's desk. Either she was braless today or the climate control made her blouse tremble. Less likely it was a wildly racing pulse because McCarry had come to flirt. "What do you think of that boy?" I asked.

"He could be a rock-video idol," she said.

"See if you can raise the Connaught Hotel in London."

I went back to my desk and watched on the quotation monitor as stock prices rambled. If I got busy I could still buy a few shares for Imrie before the market closed. Use up a hundred thousand and treat Mistress Kimball to dinner at Reggie's and champagne at Donald's. The Swiss market was closed, so the chemicals were out.

Meg buzzed, and I picked up the phone and asked for Mr. de Wohl's suite.

"One moment, please."

The next voice gave nothing away except that it might have been born female. "Madame de Wohl's suite."

"I would like to speak to Imrie de Wohl," I said. "My name is McCarry."

"I'll connect you with Madame."

Madame was more pleasant. "You're a friend of Imrie's, Mr. McCarry?"

"Not of long standing," I said. "He told me I could reach him here."

"You've missed Imrie by several days. He's in New York tonight and flies to Montreal tomorrow."

Toronto, I thought. She had a pleasant accent that could have come from anywhere.

"We were doing some business together . . ." I threw tact to the wind. "Are you his wife?"

"I am his mother." She sounded fond of the role. "Imrie has so many projects—I won't ask about this one. Can I help you further?"

"No, thank you. I'll try to reach him in Canada."

"He's at the Pierre this evening," she said.

"Thank you." Hanging up, I felt like laughing. The kid had probably inherited part of a trust fund and wanted to prove he could wreck it as fast as a bank officer.

I punched Stacy's number, then hung up. Max Oberfeld stood in the doorway, as happy as a frog with a fly in range. "That's a nice account you bagged, Rain Tree Capital. Congratulations."

He had big round eyes and short gray hair. His leer

was sexless. Though he pretended to suffer from satyriasis, and relished locker-room stories, physical sin interested Max little. A good lay was over in a minute. A stock certificate was forever.

He couldn't stand to spread unalloyed good will. "How did you land their business, promise to do the trades for three cents a share?"

"Dean Witter bid three; I had to go cheaper."

"Aggressive boy, but I like that. It's a shame you didn't leave a cut in it for yourself." He threw a prospectus onto my desk. I had already seen copies of it floating around the office. Magee & Temple was trying to sell bonds to help a moribund oil company sink more dry holes.

I lifted the document and read the glossy cover as if for the first time. "Puddyhole Exploration Corporation. It looks like an easy one to sell." I knew it was moving like week-old fish.

"I was wondering if you had seen a copy," Max said. "None of your clients seems to have bought any."

"They're not bond investors."

Max grinned. "I would expect a sharp salesman to convince them."

"Where are the sharp salesmen?" I asked.

"You could always drop a few units of this offering into the accounts you have discretion over," he said, not quite making it an order.

"Do widows and orphans come first?"

He seldom pretended to like me. He knew I must be after his job, because any ambitious man would be. He knew I was passing secret memos to Thorny Wacker. Ridiculing him to other subordinates. Scrawling his phone number in the ladies' loo. He said, "Donald, everybody in this office is expected to pull together. If there's a reason that you can't place, let's say, five thousand of the units, would you share it with me?"

35

It was pointless to argue. Instead of taking my silence as assent, he added a brilliant thought. "If all else fails you, why not put them in the Greenleaf account?"

He left and I toyed for the dozenth time with the idea of opening my own shop. Nat Gersten had gone out on his own three years ago and had four brokers working for him.

Did Nat have fewer headaches or more? When you had your own shop, it would be harder to lay off problems. On the other hand, maybe you had a clearer field to see them coming and duck.

Maybe. The Greenleaf account would have been hard to spot as trouble.

Mrs. Edna Greenleaf. Her bank in New Hampshire had opened the account with a dozen strings attached, because Mrs. Greenleaf wanted to speculate but preserve her capital. The banker said he had been referred by an investment adviser whose name meant nothing more to me than the banker's.

They had heard Magee & Temple had good bloodlines, and some lawyer in Boston I didn't remember meeting had said there was a solid fellow at the firm named McCarthy. Or maybe it had been McCarran.

The banker, Axel Windlass, thought McCarry. Axel Windlass believed in prudence the way Cotton Mather believed in penance. Buying common stocks for a seventy-six-year-old widow didn't fit New Hampshire Trust's definition of prudence. But the old biddy insisted. "Mr. Parker is adamant that the money go into stocks, so I will have to trust you not to take too many risks," Windlass said. "Perhaps we could buy some electric utilities?"

"Nuclear or coal-fired? Never mind. Who is 'Mr. Parker'?"

"He is Miss Edna's adviser. Mr. Parker has had a close relationship with New Hampshire Trust for a number of years."

That explained why Mr. Parker didn't turn Miss Edna's nest egg over directly to a broker. Doing so would have deprived Axel Windlass's bank of its half-percent custodial fee. I promised Axel I wouldn't destroy the account in the first six months. We parted with friendly mumblings. I remembered at the last moment to ask the size of the account. Eighty thousand wouldn't buy many electric utilities.

"Mr. Parker says that the amount she wishes to invest in common stocks is approximately four million." Windlass believed in making the ludicrous sound sane and inevitable. Any seventy-six-year-old who wanted to plunge that big belonged under guardianship. So did her investment adviser.

I put most of the money into utilities, just as Axel suggested, the next largest piece into preferreds, and used five hundred thousand to buy things that I thought might go up. Once in February a wheezy voice on the telephone identified itself as Roxbury Parker and congratulated me on the previous six months' results. I told him we'd had an easy market, which was true.

Miss Edna I never heard from.

A couple of months later, when Parker left a message with Meg that our client had died, my regret was abstract and impersonal. She could have been a sweetheart who baked cookies for the postman or a pisser who put Ex-Lax into Halloween bags. I'd never had a picture of her in my mind. Old farm girl or town busybody. Axel Windlass had told Meg that Miss Edna had been married to a shirtmaker.

"Mr. Parker called to say that he will be the executor," Meg said, glancing up from her notepad. "He wants you to leave the account as it is. He said we could liquidate in an orderly fashion. Her main beneficiary is a foundation."

"For pregnant cats?"

"He didn't say."

So no crepe-hanging. If I had thought about it, I would have mourned the commissions that Miss Edna took to the grave. If I'd had a small quota of second sight, I'd have mourned on my own account for the trouble she would cause.

By May, Mrs. Greenleaf's ashes were in storage waiting to make an icy New Hampshire sidewalk safe. The only fuss came from a munchkin in accounting who asked to verify a Social Security number. I turned her over to Meg and forgot about it.

Two weeks later, a slender and serious young man came around from the Internal Revenue Service. He explained that Mrs. Edna Greenleaf had not been paying her taxes. A problem for Mr. Parker, I decided, or Mr. Windlass or, that failing, Mad Max.

The young man had a small disapproving mouth and a pinched scowl that cracked his face as though someone had drawn cat whiskers across his sallow cheeks. He had started the interview trying to smile, unaware that the sneer didn't go away. The catlike traits were real enough. His blond hair was impeccably combed, lightly glossed like a well-licked pelt. His hands were delicate paws perfect for grasping small victims. He practiced a cat's seeming indifference while waiting for the mouse to come out and look around. His name was Robert Petrus.

"How long did you know Mrs. Greenleaf?" he asked.

I explained that the relationship was twice removed, through Axel Windlass and Roxbury Parker.

"You mean that Parker told you what to do?"

"He told Mr. Windlass what to do, in general terms."

"So Windlass told you what to do."

"Broadly speaking. He told me to buy Mrs. Greenleaf conservative stocks."

"I understand," Petrus said. "The government regards this inquiry as confidential. We would prefer that you not discuss it with any of the principals. If I heard you correctly, you had no direct contact with either Mrs. Greenleaf or Parker. Is that right?"

I hesitated.

He leaned forward, not so patient after all. "Is that correct or isn't it?"

I hadn't decided. Parker had spoken to Meg right after Mrs. Greenleaf's death. Did that count? Probably it did. On the other hand, Petrus's pinched expression of distaste for everything in sight didn't endear him to me. Parker had given me a verbal pat on the back. Definitely countable. But then, the voice on the phone could have belonged to an impersonator. I said, "No contact at all with Mrs. Greenleaf. One telephone call from someone who said he was Parker."

"Do you consider that unusual?"

"Not especially. There are a lot of people who don't come to New York but want to work with a New York broker. They like to feel they're in the loop."

"I suppose it's in your interest not to disabuse them," he said.

"Not especially." A meaningless response this time. I was scratching the dust with my toe.

"What about helping them evade taxes, McCarry? Is that in your interest?"

"That would be a felony."

The whiskers went through an odd spasm. "More than one stockbroker has gone to jail in the last year."

"Any tax-motivated trades we execute are legal," I said. "Do you have any more questions about the Greenleaf account?"

"I may."

"Then ask them, so I can get on with my work."

He shook his head. "I'll conduct this interview at my own pace."

I said nothing.

"Was this the first time you had an account for Mrs. Greenleaf?"

"Yes."

"What about other clients of Parker or Windlass?"

"This was the first."

"How did they happen to come to you?"

A very, very good question. "Windlass said Parker had heard about me from someone."

"That's conveniently vague."

"It happens that way. This was a lawyer or another broker in Boston—something like that. Sears doesn't ask who told you to buy a refrigerator from them."

"I find it hard to believe that you had a client you never talked to," Petrus said. "Who then, conveniently, died."

We were back to that. I pondered responses, swallowed them all.

Petrus said, "You don't look like an especially credulous man."

"Go piss in your hat," I said.

He went straight to Mad Max, who confirmed that I was a Communist and tax dodger. Max reported this with relish. "The old woman probably forgot to pay last year's taxes," he said. "Now they want to bring her back from the dead to do time. God bless 'em."

I wondered why, if Agent Petrus knew Miss Edna hadn't paid taxes, the account hadn't been frozen.

7

I ROLLED THROUGH THE COMPUTER LIST OF CLIENTS, LOOK-
ing for victims.

Five million worth of Puddyhole Exploration
wasn't too big an assignment. But it posed a tactical
dilemma. I could dump it into four or five big
accounts, where it wouldn't make a splash. But the big
accounts were likely to hold it against me when
Puddyhole stopped paying interest. Or I could spread
it through a hundred or so individual accounts and
hope that all the owners followed Mrs. Greenleaf to
the grave before Puddyhole did. The survivors might
forget that they hadn't asked for a piece of this one.

I went out and traded jokes with Timmy Upham.
We had heard the same ones from the same source.
Two dogs at the vet, one for peeing on the rug, one for
raping his mistress. Which gets terminated, which gets
its nails trimmed? Timmy went back to his desk. I got
a cup of hot water and eyed Meg speculatively. Had
her eyes lingered on Timmy as we yukked over the
news wire?

I closed the office door behind me.

Phone on my shoulder, I found a number in my
card file and browsed a few pages of Puddyhole
Exploration's prospectus while listening to the rings.

A voice answered impatiently. "Lippert!"

"It's Don McCarry," I said. I waited.

Terrence Lippert's pipe clicked against his teeth.
"Ah, McCarry! How are you?"

41

"There's something interesting making the rounds. If we're absolutely off the record—all the way off—I might fill you in."

"I'm kind of swamped right now."

"I understand." I did, too. Nobody calls a reporter out of charity. If I was on the phone, I had an ax to grind. For listening, he wanted at least one very loud smack on the ass. I puckered up and delivered. "I wanted someone who's a whiz at numbers to have first crack at this."

We agreed to meet at the Harvey House after the market closed.

"You know, I wanted to get together with you anyway," Terrence Lippert said. He looked well dressed and at the same time unkempt. The tweedy gray suit and paisley tie were crisp, but his hair was reddish-brown straw poking in odd directions. He had staked out the last stool in the bar, which was jammed with traders from the block houses at the toe of Broadway. Whether the markets had closed up or down, it was a jubilant crowd because everyone had been prescient and shorted stocks or gone long on Deutsche marks or vice versa or managed some other fiddle. Most of the faces jumping around us were in their twenties, with a rare gray head belonging to someone who had failed to move up and away. The older fellows were the loudest, offering their experience to kids who knew that any wisdom more than two hours old was useless.

I didn't mind standing at attention while Terrence sat, but I wanted a booth's seclusion. We walked around a tall glass partition etched with kings and queens and got a cramped table. I snagged a waitress and ordered something for myself. Terrence asked for another gimlet.

I unfolded a copy of the Puddyhole Exploration prospectus. "Take a look at this."

He drew the little document over with a fingertip. "That's your firm's name on the bottom, Magee & Temple. They're underwriting the issue."

"Yes."

"So you want me to write something nice about it."

"I didn't say that. I just thought you might find the fine print interesting."

He flipped through a couple of pages, then folded the prospectus and slipped it into his jacket. How much he understood depended on how lazy he was. The dirt on management's greed and ineptitude was well buried. He would need a couple of hours to excavate the footnotes. "I'll look it over," he said. "Now it's my turn. I hear that you've hit it off with Gustav Raab. I'm still interested in him, and I'm looking for sources. Nothing would be on the record."

"I can't imagine where you got the idea we hit it off," I said.

"Patrick Squires."

"I can't imagine where he got it."

Lippert slipped a pipe stem between his teeth and with a few clicks and slurs said, "You certainly made a beeline for Raab at the Portfolio Club."

"I did my best," I conceded. "The guy brushes off brokers like lint. Have you talked to Lucius Astenberg?"

"Senile old bastard won't see me."

He couldn't be that senile. "You sound determined. Is there something that makes Raab a hot story?"

"Not really. Just a relatively new face in town. *Fortune* hasn't done him. He doesn't get quoted in the newspapers. Let's say he's fresh. The next time I have to phone Robert Stovall for a quote I'm going to throw a fit."

"Why do you use him?"

"He's quite good about answering his phone. We create 'experts,' you know, by quoting them repeatedly. The process is mutually beneficial. Nonentities

43

become authorities, and they're *our* authorities, aren't they?"

"It's too bad that Raab doesn't make himself accessible," I said.

"He could be totally full of shit too. But until I know that for certain, he's worth cultivating." He raised his gimlet. "Portrait of a man in search of an oracle."

I raised my drink. "Best of luck. Have you ever used Thornton Wacker?"

"The head of your firm? Thorny Wacker? Oh— what a thought! My managing editor would know I've turned to satire."

"He dresses well," I protested.

"Yes, he does, doesn't he? But the man's a total idiot. I think he must have some special skill with the old ladies. Your firm rather caters to people who've lost most of their teeth, doesn't it?"

"We like to think of it as seasoned money."

"Oh yes."

"What about Astenberg? He should be quotable."

"I told you, he won't see me. Besides, he's got to be round the bend. The man must be eighty-five."

"I wonder how he knows Raab?"

"They are rather different generations, aren't they?"

"And Raab has been based in Europe."

Lippert shrugged. "I'll try to find someone who knows them both." He changed the subject. "The market was off rather sharply in the last hour, wouldn't you say? If I sold stocks for a living, action like that would make me nervous that the roof might be about to cave in."

"A good broker can find reasons for optimism even then. The roof-replacement business would be booming."

"But seriously—you're not worried?"

44

"You haven't decided to make me a famous oracle?"

"Not a chance. I'm just sampling the working man's opinion."

"There isn't much to worry about. The country's business isn't booming, and it isn't dying in its tracks. It's just plodding along, and you can plod for a long time without getting into trouble. Stock prices haven't been going crazy, so there aren't the excesses that need to be washed out." Thinking about Magee & Temple's hope that investors would swallow Puddyhole Exploration, I wondered if excesses weren't beginning to creep in.

He pushed back his wild hair and looked for our waitress. He was a man in the middle. He didn't like stockbrokers but needed them. If he wrote an article that made Terrence Lippert sound astute at the expense of the men and women he quoted, then he had achieved exactly the right balance of fact and malice. He had burned Timmy Upham in print several years ago, and Timmy still complained at neighborhood watering holes to anyone who would listen.

Did Terrence consider his promise that we were off the record binding? If he discovered that I had lied about doing business with Raab, he might consider a hatchet job on Puddyhole with my name attached to it fitting punishment.

"How long has Raab been in New York?" I asked.

"Eighteen months, approximately. He may have had a presence over here longer than that through intermediaries. It's damn difficult to find out who he does business with. Raab Capital is technically based in Geneva. Rain Tree Capital is registered in the Netherlands Antilles. Raab himself lived in Paris, where the firm used to have an office. My sources on the Continent"—he put a little air on the phrase—"say Raab is low-key over there. It's probably all posturing, don't you think? A lot of firms recruit business by pretending to be too exclusive for their clientele. Your Thorny Wacker has the right idea, old money, young money, it's all the same."

"The old money has better manners."

He looked around, leaned toward me. "People get into trouble entrusting their money to firms that are all image. You remember the Hudson Inn Capital Group, of course? This little ferret named Lisker set the thing up five years ago, claiming direct lineage from Ichabod Crane or somebody like that. He attracted money because none of the gentry wanted to admit that they hadn't been doing business with such an old-line firm all along. Shorting currencies and Treasury bills, Lisker ran through eighty million dollars in seven months. Remarkable, don't you agree?"

8

STACY LEFT WORK EARLY ON FRIDAY. WE SPENT A LEISURE-ly Saturday morning in bed. For lunch we found an open-air restaurant on the border of the East Village. Punk was waning, if you judged by the number of passing weirdos, and gentrification was chic. If they were artists and playwrights, they chased a muse who wore five-hundred-dollar unconstructed jackets. I wondered how many had progressed to buying stocks and annuities.

Ms. Kimball had turned introspective to the point of being unreachable. For some reason I made an effort. "You were showing signs of life an hour ago," I said, leaving it to her to remember she had been thrashing and mewling.

She didn't look around. "You always know the right thing to say."

"I seldom do," I said.

"You don't even make a good stab at it."

"If you plan to catalog my faults, start with insensitivity."

Her face came around from the street. At unpredictable moments, she insisted on being taken seriously. Frivolous talk was banished until urgent things had been discussed. Like whether I took my work and my life seriously enough. There is a little bit of the busybody from the neighborhood improvement society in every woman. Being improved was part of the price you paid for being in her neighborhood.

"Sometimes, Donald," she said evenly between tiny, exquisite teeth, "I have trouble believing you're an adult."

"When I have doubts, I just accept them and plod along."

She shook her head in despair. For a moment I expected her to break from the table and stalk off, confident that a Saturday without her couldn't be enjoyed. Instead she grabbed a red-bound menu. "Let's order. Dad wants me to bring you up tomorrow."

"All right."

"He said he needed a distant eye's appraisal of a situation. He wouldn't tell me what."

"Keeping secrets isn't very adult of him," I said.

"That's the only thing you have in common."

"We both adore you."

"You don't adore me. You like to take me over the jumps in bed. And maybe you like the company, when you haven't got something else on your mind."

"That's not true—or it isn't all of it."

"And even that's not what pisses me off. What

47

really gets me is that your view of the future ends somewhere around next Thursday afternoon."

Charles Kimball looked as though he had chased a few young things down the boardwalk. Probably he hadn't told his daughter about those races—or about the ones he had caught. She would never believe that Mrs. Kimball hadn't been the only love in Charlie's life.

Of course he looked ahead—as his grandfather had. You don't put together a Tracer Minerals Corporation by getting jittery when a week-old investment hasn't paid off. But until he had built his stake, the founding Kimball had surely practiced hustling and scrounging. You needed today's dime to beget tomorrow's million.

I fiddled with my menu and conceded, "I could afford a longer view, I guess." With patience, I would still own my Presto-Wok and be ahead a few grand instead of in the hole. If I thought ahead, I wouldn't have told an IRS agent to piss in his hat. With patience, I would be pushing stocks for Magee & Temple on my fiftieth birthday. Raising a water glass, I gave patience the weak toast it deserved.

Patience hadn't gotten me Gustav Raab's business.

9

WE REACHED THE CAUSEWAY THAT CONNECTED CHARLIE Kimball's Waubeeka Island to the Connecticut coast. "He didn't raise the drawbridge, so I guess you're still invited," Stacy said. She gunned the red Porsche across a steel-mesh span that could be lifted from the island side. If capitalism ever lost out on the mainland, Charlie could run his ten acres according to John Galt's rulebook.

An entourage of nanny, housekeeper, little sister, and daddy turned out on the driveway. "You're in time for breakfast," Charlie Kimball said. He was small and dapper, white-haired and almost dashing in pale blue ducks and a matching sweater that showed up his tan. Betsy Kimball was a green-twig version of her sister, at seventeen all legs and brown hair and maturing grace. The girls hugged, Charlie and Stacy hugged, and I got a surprisingly sincere handshake. "Thank you for coming," he said.

I looked around. Stacy was twenty feet ahead. He'd said it to me.

"You're welcome."

"Stacy told you I wanted your opinion on something?"

"You didn't tell her what."

"Actually, I was misleading both of you a trifle."

Breakfast was held on a second-floor screened porch overlooking the water. Fifty yards off the island's east point, a day sailer had turned its nose into the tide. On the lawn gulls squatted on a high spot that caught the sun.

Betsy sat next to me. "We don't see you very often, Donald." She wore a pink sundress, white sandals, and tiny lavender shell earrings. Her fingers were long and tanned, unadorned except for a pair of scraped knuckles. Perhaps a boyfriend had gotten too intense.

"Staying out of the market's way has kept me busy," I said.

"Are you making money?"

"I bought a new necktie yesterday."

She smiled. "A good week, then. Daddy hasn't bought a new necktie since I was born. Have you?"

"I bought a new razor last week," he said, patting his cheek. "Necessities take precedence."

"You are a skinflint, sweetheart," Stacy said.

"You don't know," her sister said. "He's got us rebuilding the rock wall. He even had Willie working on it yesterday."

Willie was a gardener who must have been seventy. Stacy looked at her father dubiously. "I hope not."

"William wanted to help, so I let him supervise. You didn't see him levering any stones around, did you, Bets?"

"You left that to me."

Charlie Kimball poured himself coffee, looked from one girl to the other. "I can't count on you two to help sink new pilings at the pier? What about you, Donald—a couple of weekends in the country?"

"I eat better than I work."

"So it's Willie, I'm afraid. The work will be slower than I had hoped. William isn't as efficient as he was twenty years ago."

"Where's Matthew Josephson when you need him?" Stacy asked.

We finished breakfast, and Betsy took me to see the wall. It hemmed in a pasture that was overgrown with blackberry bushes. We stayed in the grass on the other side. What I knew about rock-wall building wouldn't have impressed anyone, but walking its perimeter I gathered that the repairs were less arduous than the girls and their father had let on. None of the stones that had fallen away was bigger than a football.

"It's pretty solid all in all," Betsy said. She sat on a flat ledge. "Gravity holds it together. Provided you've built it right, of course. See—the stones tilt inward from each side." She reached around and pointed. "If you use mortar it comes loose and you have to replace it. This is more scientific. Leave it to the Kimballs to hire gravity to work for them. At least the price is right."

"Your father is a tough customer," I said.

"Hell on wheels," she agreed. "He's afraid poor

Willie is getting bored and losing his faculties, so he keeps inventing projects for him."

"Do you know why he invited me up here today?"

"No. He's usually not friendly toward any of his daughters' men." She stretched a leg and stared at her brown toes. As she bent to flick a burr from her sandal strap, the sundress drooped. Apart from turning away or looking somewhere else, I didn't have much choice but a lingering inspection of a small bare breast. The nipple looked unfinished and vulnerable.

She straightened up. "Actually, you're one of the few Stacy has brought home. Except for Sterling, and that was ages ago. She must like you a lot."

"It's mutual," I said.

She stood up and brushed the back of her skirt. "If you're not blown away by the wall, we can look for dead things on the beach."

"That sounds good."

The gulls had gotten to the best stuff. We found a couple of ripe mullets and a horseshoe crab, abandoned by a tide rushing out to the Sound.

"There are ducks down by the causeway," Betsy said, "whole families puttering around. Did you see them when you came across?"

"No."

"If we get a chance later, I'll show you—unless you've had enough of the nature walk."

"I could stand ducks."

"Okay, but we'd better get back." She paused and looked at me solemnly. Her round face opened into a grin. "If Daddy asked you up, you're in for it somehow."

Charlie Kimball was complaining on the telephone because a local bank was offering its depositors a portfolio of low-quality, high-yield bonds. "It's just irresponsible, and I told Louis so. I even threatened to resign from the board. Some of these goddamned

51

companies that issued the bonds aren't going to be alive in five years, let alone alive and making interest payments." He heard us on the steps and asked over his shoulder, "Isn't that right, Donald?"

He didn't wait for an answer. He slammed the receiver down. "This hot dog down in Stamford has patched together a little conglomerate with twenty times as much debt as equity. Come a recession, he's dead. So are the chumps holding his bonds. Right, Donald?"

"It sounds risky," I agreed.

"It's worse than risky, it's reckless."

I said, "Of course, your hot dog has built his business faster than he could have without borrowing. And if he can repay some of the debt before a recession hits, he might survive."

"You're talking the patter of a gambler."

Perspective was everything. The leveragers wanted to get rich. So they accepted big risks—and invited in anyone willing to share the danger knowingly or innocently. Charlie Kimball wanted to stay rich. That dictated small risks.

Stacy interrupted. "Don has to talk stocks five days a week. Give him a break."

The breakfast dishes were gone, and Charlie had stretched out on a padded steamer chair with a travel magazine across his belly. But he wasn't in a reading mood. "It was good of you to come up, Donald. Can Stace get you a drink?"

"It's a little early."

"A soft drink then."

I looked at her. "A Coke?"

She shrugged. "Sounds possible. Come along. You hold the glass, I'll pour."

We didn't go to the kitchen. There was a small octagonal brick building out back where Stacy had set up a studio the previous summer, when she was painting. It was littered with canvases, paints, and stiffened brushes and looked as though the interest had been abandoned between lunch and dinner. "When Daddy starts offering you booze before noon, be careful," she said, closing the door. "Cripes, what a mess! I wish I had more time."

She straightened up a workbench for a while, lining up paints, scraping a palette, pouring turpentine onto brushes that she said were beyond rescue. "Sorry that we're wasting a day like this. There are probably better things to do."

"I've got the time," I said.

They showed up after lunch, bumping across the causeway in a dusty white sedan. We had played Scrabble, we had talked about movies and politics, we had compared the rapaciousness of Magee & Temple and the Hammer Gallery. Now we were going to get down to business.

"I invited some friends over," Charlie said.

As they climbed out, uncomfortable in short-sleeved shirts and polyester slacks, they didn't look like anybody's friends. There was my stringy friend with the pinched face from the IRS, Petrus. The older one accompanying him had a grim mouth-set. He could have been a cancer patient whose painkiller had faded. My bet made him a civil servant with a mission. He had very short hair, a deep tan, large hands, and a gold watch that flashed brightly at fifty feet. His shirt was a blue gingham that still had store creases. By the time I noticed the creases, he was shaking hands with Charlie on the porch steps. It was too late to hide behind a pot of geraniums. I stood with my hands in my back pockets, trading stares with Stacy. She looked convincingly put off.

"Greg, how nice to see you," Charlie said. "We were having lemonade, but could I offer you something stronger? Is this Mr. Petrus? Girls, this is an old friend, Greg Lord, and his associate, Bob Petrus." Charlie backed away, and the porch got crowded. It was a big porch, fifty feet long, with a glider at one end, a wicker set at the other, and room for scrimmages in between. But it still felt crowded with Greg aboard.

He offered his hand to Stacy. "It's always a pleasure."

She asked bluntly, "Have we met?"

"Not since you were in high school. Is this Elizabeth?" She was out of reach behind the table, so he waved.

I was within reach. When he stuck out a hand, I folded my arms. He nodded. "Bob said you weren't friendly."

Charlie Kimball was counting on me to be civil. To hell with him. "I've got my prejudices," I said. First and foremost, against ball-squeezers from the public payroll. No point in specifying that. I wouldn't reform Lord or Petrus.

"Agent Petrus concedes that he got off on the wrong foot with you," Lord said. "There may have been misunderstandings on both sides. I think we can clear them up."

I didn't answer.

He said gravely, "There are no hard feelings on the government's part."

Charlie Kimball put on a big grin. "I knew that would be your attitude, Greg. Don doesn't bear any either, I'll wager."

Don kept his mouth shut.

"The slate's clean," Lord said. All they needed were boaters and canes.

"In the interest of furthering our new friendship," I said, "tell me how you got Mr. Kimball to set up this meeting."

Greg Lord clapped his big hands. "It's real simple, Don. When you were unresponsive to Agent Petrus's questions about the Greenleaf account, he wondered if you were hiding something. He went to see your office manager, Mr. Oberfeld, who added to his doubts. Oberfeld implied that you wouldn't be above laundering criminal money."

"Or above anything else," Petrus piped up.

They were waiting for a response. I said, "That sounds about right."

"So the government looked further, or rather Bob's department did," Lord said.

"Bob's department is the Internal Revenue Service," I said. "What's yours?"

"We both work for the Treasury," Greg Lord said. "Anyway, when we looked into your background, we found you were spanking clean. A model citizen. None of your clients had obvious pieces of unexplained income. Neither you nor they seemed to have ties to any crime families. When Bob's people showed me a list of your associates, Stacy Kimball's name jumped right out. I asked Charlie if he thought a less formal approach to you might be productive. He was happy to oblige."

They traded looks like pats on the back. Once they explained it to the dummy, he was bound to want to help. I told him, "Okay, thanks. I was just curious." I turned to Stacy. "Are you ready to head back to town?"

Lord's face stiffened. "You haven't heard what I've got to say, Don."

"I've heard enough to look twice at Charlie Kimball's next invitation. What you've got to say doesn't interest me."

"You talk like you think you're a tough guy."

"Not very. I just don't feel like helping you collect Uncle Sam's estate taxes."

Lord shook his head. "It's got nothing to do with estate taxes. The problem is with the client, Mrs. Greenleaf. Did you have many conversations with her?"

At the bottom step, I hesitated. They were on that again. "Conversations with her? Not that I recall. The account was handled by a money manager."

"Yes, with a bank custodian along the way," Lord said. He looked significantly at Charlie. "It's an odd thing, but the custodian, Mr. Axel Windlass, didn't have many talks with Mrs. Greenleaf either. As a matter of fact, none at all. What about you, Don?"

"What are you getting at?"

"We don't think Mrs. Greenleaf ever existed."

The afternoon had gotten warm. We were sitting, Stacy and I on the railing, Greg Lord and Petrus at the wicker table, and Charlie on a dining room chair he had brought out. Betsy had gotten bored and wandered off. Charlie and Petrus were swigging lemonade, Stacy a gin and tonic, Lord a glass of water. I wished I had taken Charlie up on a beer. Lord's story had begun to interest me.

"When you bought or sold stock for the Greenleaf account," he said to me, "your office had three places to send confirmations of the trades. A copy went to Axel Windlass at the bank in New Hampshire. Another copy went to her financial adviser, Roxbury Parker. The third was addressed to Mrs. Greenleaf herself. Did you realize that the address for the woman was a post office box in Merrimack, New Hampshire? As far as we can find, Mrs. Greenleaf had no actual residence in the town. At least there is no telephone listing or tax bill for her. We did find a record of her death, registered with the county, certified by an attending physician. The body was cremated."

"Wouldn't there be an address on the death certificate?" Charlie asked.

"There was one in Tampa, Florida. A wealthy old lady wouldn't be caught dead in that building."

"Have you tried those facts out on Axel Windlass or Roxbury Parker?" I said.

"We don't want to. We're satisfied that our information is good. Widow Greenleaf was a cutout. We even know basically how it was done. There was a child named Edna Greenleaf who died in the early sixties in Newburyport, Massachusetts. Cross-referencing of births and deaths doesn't go back far. With a copy of the kid's birth certificate from the courthouse, someone could get a passport, a Social Security number, all sorts of documentation to set up an identity. Once they've created a person, changing details isn't hard. The person for the passport can be a thirty-year-old. That's useful if you're flying people around South America. But the Edna Greenleaf who opens bank accounts can be a seventyish widow."

"It sounds hard to catch," Stacy said.

Lord nodded. "Bob Petrus's agency keeps trying to close the hidey-holes. They've implemented software that takes the reports brokerage firms and banks file on customer transactions and cross-checks them with taxpayers' own reports, Social Security claims, federal grant applications, student loans—quite a few things. We're making the social net tighter every year. One of those computer screens threw out Edna Greenleaf. Some things didn't quite mesh."

"What things?" Stacy said.

"That's Agent Petrus's department. Bob?"

Petrus shook his head. "They don't need to know that."

Lord shrugged. "It doesn't matter anyway. When we began checking, the pattern all of a sudden looked familiar."

"So Petrus came around asking questions."

"That wasn't handled very well. We intended our interest to be sub rosa. When Robert alienated you without really learning anything, there was a chance you would get on the phone and ask Roxbury Parker why the IRS was snooping around. That would have been a wipeout. You didn't, did you?"

"No."

"I didn't think so." Greg Lord glanced down at his paws to hide a look of relief. "What about the banker, Windlass?"

"I didn't talk to him either."

"I'm glad to hear that."

"Something bothers me. The IRS has a reputation for being aggressive in its collections. Yet you haven't frozen the Greenleaf account."

"No point in spooking the game," Lord said. "If the money goes anywhere, we'll know about it. As for Parker and Windlass, I understand you don't have any other accounts with them. Do you know anyone on the Street they work with regularly?"

I shook my head and explained how the business had come down from Boston.

"I'll tell you what we would like from you, Don," Greg Lord said. I had volunteered something and that encouraged him. "Would you stay in touch with Parker, maybe cultivate his business? I don't know how brokers do that sort of thing—"

I volunteered again. "We feed the suckers ideas. The first couple are free, with a hint that another is in the works. I imply that the new thing looks pretty good. But naturally, I've got to give it to my clients first. The stock is a little thin and might run as word gets out. If the prospect wants to call back in a few weeks . . . Most of them get the message."

"You could do something like that with Parker, and he might bite?"

"Mrs. Greenleaf's account made money, so he should be happy with me."

"Good, good."

"What will you learn if he brings me a few more accounts?"

"We'll have a better idea of how much money he has to launder."

"Are you certain that's what he's doing?"

"At the very least, he's evading taxes. The Greenleaf job was a classic. Four million bucks goes from being footloose and dirty to being part of a New Hampshire widow's estate."

Laundering or evading taxes for whom? I almost asked, just to prompt Petrus to say I didn't need to know.

"Are you ready now for a beer?" Charlie Kimball asked. He grinned from me to Greg Lord, as if we were both reliable son-in-law material. We were getting on splendidly, he must have thought.

"Beer sounds just right," Lord said.

"I'll pass," I replied. "So, Greg, you and Bob are satisfied that I'm not in cahoots with Parker in the money-washing business."

"We never really thought you were," Lord said. "Charlie assured me that once we had explained everything—"

"Old Don McCarry would sign up for the home team," I finished for him. "You've explained fine. But it doesn't change anything. I still don't give a damn whether you collect your taxes or not."

The silence was drawn out. Greg Lord looked inward, thumb-indexing through the Treasury Department manual on civilian relations, which said that if you confided in the taxpayer and shared a beer afterward, the good citizen would fall over himself to help the government maintain law and order. He had been nice and hadn't forgotten the beer. The manual couldn't be wrong. So what was?

Petrus cracked a nasty smile. He had known all along that Citizen McCarry was a bad egg.

I embarrassed everybody on the porch by breaking the impasse. "I mean, I don't feel like helping you for free—as a patriotic gesture or anything like that."

Charlie Kimball blushed. He had invited a hustler to be bamboozled. Stacy rolled her eyes.

For the first time, Greg Lord smiled. "There is a bounty on any illicit funds that the Treasury recovers. You would be entitled to a percentage."

We stared at each other for a moment.

"We can put the details in writing," he said.

10

THEY DIDN'T STAY FOR ANY OF CHARLIE'S BEER.

Stacy went inside, and Kimball came back to the porch. "Did you do that because I put you on the spot?"

"Partly. Also because I didn't like them."

"Greg will look harder at your background. I hope there is nothing to be found."

"Nothing he can use." I hoped I was right. Corruption of the blood was forbidden somewhere in the Constitution, wasn't it?

Kimball leaned back. "Thinking you're pretty important comes with collecting a public paycheck. I did it for a while during the war, and I know. Working under Ken Galbraith in the price-control office, I got so I liked having businessmen kiss my ass for a two-percent price rise that would keep them alive. I was just out of Yale and knew I was saving the country. My father almost disowned me."

I nodded.

"When I came into the family business," he said, "I saw what the old man had been complaining about. Government works to government's ends, not necessarily mine or yours. Greg Lord hasn't had the opportunity to understand that and probably won't. He's career Treasury. Catching bad people is his rationale in life. You don't seem to care about bad people. Is that just a pose?"

"There's no point in this," I said.

"I might satisfy my curiosity about you. I don't entertain any notion that you're a criminal. But do you really not care what this Parker fellow is up to?" He leaned forward, bright-eyed as an ichthyologist expecting a fish to speak.

"It looks like he's breaking a couple of laws," I said. "If anyone can figure out which ones, he'll probably go to jail. If they can't figure out which ones, they can always RICO him with a blanket charge of general criminality. That will make the world spick-and-span and help the career of whichever U.S. attorney prosecutes the case."

"I see . . ." He was silent, no longer looking at me. "Well, let's go find out whether my daughter is still speaking to you. If Stacy isn't, Elizabeth will, I suppose."

We walked through the sparely furnished hall. None of the Kimball ancestors glowered from the walls to remind the grandson he hadn't achieved it all by himself. Despite its age the house was sunny and open, a place for comfortable summers rather than a monument to an overbearing fortune. In good weather, Charlie Kimball spent most of his days conducting business by telephone from an upstairs porch. A couple of times a week, according to Stacy, he drove into Stamford, where Tracer Minerals had its headquarters. More often the senior vice president, a sister's thirty-year-old son, brought out any papers that needed instant attention. Charlie's restlessness kept the phone lines going and the young vice president on the road.

Betsy intercepted us on her way downstairs. "Boy, are you on Stacy's shit list!"

Kimball sighed. "Don't worry, Donald. She'll get over it."

"What do you mean by 'Donald'?" Betsy said. "You're the one she's furious at, Daddy. What did you do?"

"Just arranged a little business, sweetheart."

"It must have been some skulduggery. The family's good at it."

When I got back to town I found another copy of Magee & Temple's offering prospectus for Puddyhole Exploration and mailed it without comment to Kimball. A few days later I got a note back.

Donald:
    If I read your message correctly, you say, 'What is money laundering compared to a license to steal?' Point taken.

Regards,
Charlie

I put the note away and speculated unproductively on Charlie's lingering ties to the government. Most businessmen didn't play matchmaker for the Treasury Department's snoopers. Those who did got something back. Given the breadth of Tracer Minerals' empire, I supposed Charlie Kimball could collect a lot of favors for his help. It was only reflex crotchetiness—and Bolshevism, as Mad Max would testify—that made me suspect that Tracer's interests and the government's got blurred fairly often.

On that unworthy thought, I went back to watching the market. Timmy Upham had been grousing because he had gotten a quota on a new deal. "Not Puddyhole," he informed me. "This is the First Italian Income Fund—can you believe it? Two hundred million we hope to raise, and what do you think Magee & Temple's management fee will be for sitting on a pile of Italian interest-bearing paper? One and a half million a year, every year. Am I supposed to tell my clients this is good for them?"

"Tell them it fits into the big picture," I suggested.

"What big picture?"

"Concentrating capital in the hands of those worthy to hold it."

He found that unhelpful and left.

And how much, I wondered, did Roxbury Parker earn by creating widows who didn't live long? Did he pocket a million and a half a year for that service to his real clients . . . whoever they were?

Greg Lord had implied organized crime. A broad heading these days.

Meg Sorkin was shuffling account forms when I went out to her square. Timmy Upham's door was closed. So were Art Bradshaw's and Isaiah Stern's. Mine had been. "Where are your admirers?" I asked.

"Holed up with their frustrations. You haven't had much to say lately, either. If it's any consolation, Mr. Oberfeld is out of the office until Thursday."

"It's a lot of consolation. Have you heard what he's doing?"

"No."

Two years ago another firm had tried to recruit him away from Magee & Temple. Max had parlayed the offer into a bigger bonus. A mild hope stirred in me that someone had found his price.

"Could you pull the paperwork on Mrs. Greenleaf?" I said.

She dug into the line of low file cabinets where the four brokers' business was mingled. I skimmed the Greenleaf form for the phone number of the investment adviser, R. B. Parker Counsel, Ltd. The space was blank. The address was a post office box in Merrimack, New Hampshire. The names of Axel Windlass and New Hampshire Trust were there on separate lines. I went into my office, phoned Windlass, beat around the bush for a minute, and then got Roxbury Parker's phone number.

Then I hesitated. If Parker ran a laundry service for a local crime family, I didn't want to cross him.

But did I believe what Greg Lord had implied? I didn't believe that Lord would instinctively tell the whole truth about whether the sun was shining.

I punched the number.

Without even a brush with a secretary, I got Mr. Roxbury Parker. He had a wheezy Yankee voice, half familiar from his brief pat-on-the-back call. He was at least middle-aged, I thought, possibly much older.

"Mr. McCarry? Oh, my young broker friend! How are you, young man?"

"Quite well, Mr. Parker. We were sorry to hear about Mrs. Greenleaf."

"Oh, oh! Yes, we were saddened too. She was an unusual woman, quite peculiar. Perhaps 'remarkable' would be a better word."

"I'm sorry that I never got a chance to meet her."

"Edna was reclusive, Mr. McCarry. Especially since her husband died, she seldom ventured far from Merrimack."

I didn't ask about dives in Florida. "How long had she been a widow?"

"Oh, dear. For longer than I knew her." He wheezed and fell silent.

"There's another reason I called," I said. "We haven't gotten instructions to close out the account—"

"Oh, no! There's no hurry about that. Mrs. Greenleaf left most of her estate to charities. I believe probate will be swift. As executor I see no reason to disturb profitable securities positions any sooner than necessary. The prime beneficiary agrees. They have indicated they will leave the bequest under my management. That means, in turn, that the account will remain with you."

"I looked through the account today," I said. "A couple of the stocks have gone up about as far as we can expect. I think they should be sold. I couldn't do anything without touching base with you."

"Which stocks would they be?"

I mentioned two that had gone up decently.

He hemmed. "I defer to your judgment, sir. Let them go!"

"I'll take care of it." I drew a long breath and made my pitch. "There is a small company up your way that one of our analysts has been following. It's exciting—not suitable for an estate. I wondered if you might be interested for other clients?"

He gave a reedy chuckle. "I'm always interested in good ideas, Mr. McCarry. Tell me about it."

I spun him a story about a company called Dairy Drive-Ins, based on Cape Cod. A fast-growing franchiser indistinguishable from a dozen others. I had our research report in front of me and dropped a couple of details that made me sound on a first-name basis with Dairy Drive-Ins' president.

"Intriguing," Roxbury Parker said. "Perhaps I could be convinced. In fact, I might entrust some funds to you on a discretionary basis. We have a couple of small investment pools."

"We could make some money," I said. That should be all there was to it. I would count the zeros on the check he sent.

"I would like," Parker whistled, "to talk with you at greater length about the kinds of investments you will be making. Your handling of Edna's account was just exemplary. She was most appreciative. But I'm always eager for more information, quite a pest about it, I'm afraid."

"That's no problem."

"This kind of thing would be better done in a face-to-face discussion. I wonder if it would be possible for you to come up here? Naturally I would pay your expenses."

I'd have sooner gone skinny-dipping with Max.

He said, "I'm at an age where I have a problem getting around."

Wishing I had bargained harder with Lord, I said, "I suppose I could take a day."

"You might have to make it an overnight trip, but we've got a nice inn. Could you come up on Thursday?"

I put him on hold and asked Meg, "When is Max due back?"

"Thursday."

We made an appointment for two P.M. at his office. He gave me directions. I had to fly to Logan, then take a commuter hop. Then rent a car.

Meg made the arrangements. There weren't any late afternoon flights back. She booked me into the Merrimack Inn.

"Do we have any prospectuses left for Puddyhole?" I asked.

She rolled open a cabinet drawer and pointed to the stack. "Take as many as you want. Mr. Bradshaw brought his back. He said something I'd better not repeat."

"I won't tell."

"He said he'd rather fit a diaphragm on an elephant." She barely blushed. "I don't think he'll put it that way to Mr. Oberfeld."

According to the brokers' motivational expert that Thorny Wacker brought in, if you talk to only twenty-five people a day your business is dying. "How can you get two or three new referrals at that pace?" the supersalesman demanded. "If you don't get three leads a day, you won't be bringing in ten clients a month. If you can't do that, you aren't worth your desk space."

My client list wasn't dying. Mad Max's scowling visits notwithstanding, I wasn't ready to admit that. I did my clients no more harm than I could help, and there was a core of people who had stayed with me for years and had made a little money. But the business had plateaued in the last year. My enthusiasm had waned, partly as the vision of Don McCarry as a heavy hitter on Wall Street had faded. I was thirty-eight years old and was gradually accepting that the future wouldn't be much different from the past. With moderate diligence I would earn a living three rungs better than the national average. But the loft in SoHo and an occasional weekend in the Bahamas kept the income and expenses just about even. There was no big score in the future, no picture on the cover of *Investor's Week*.

No burning urge to chase the odd client for an order.

But I spent much of the afternoon on the telephone anyway. The market was up and people wanted to buy. A retired longshoreman in Queens told me to pick up as much of a down-and-out air-freight company as I could get under nine dollars a share. I got thirty-five hundred shares before somebody noticed the action and joined in, bumping the price to nine and an eighth. All over the country medium-sized retail accounts wanted to jump on moving trains.

Bill Hinsdale called from Europe while I was in the library. It was late evening in Paris, and he told Meg he was going out.

I punched up the code for Electronics Corporation of Belgium and found it was up another two points today. That took the price to forty-eight dollars a share, about sixty percent above the level when Bill had tipped me. The company had gotten its international contract. Gustav Raab had phoned a few days earlier to say that he had noticed that my idea was working out profitably. I wondered what I could send Bill as thanks.

11

ROXBURY PARKER'S HEALTH HAD RALLIED, AT LEAST FOR the afternoon. He was a gangly Yankee with a long jaw and flat face, dingy white hair and nicotined eyebrows. His seersucker suit could have been bought the spring forty years ago when he left college. But his handshake was hard. "We're out of the stream of things up here," he said, giving me a long stare at worn-flat teeth. His voice was high and lungy. "You can fill me in on New York's fads. Just the investment stuff. I don't want to hear about raw fish."

I told him that that one had passed.

We left his office in a clapboard building on Main Street that also housed a general store. Commerce in Merrimack seemed to depend heavily on sports shops, hotels, and antiques emporiums. We walked up a geranium-trimmed side street with a bare mountain slope lurking behind the roofs. Parker's stride was loose, and he wore an aimless grin. He told me, "Your hotel has the only decent restaurant in town. Chef's from *Baws*-ton. I thought we would eat there."

He seemed at ease with himself, without a clue that the Treasury was looking over his shoulder, sending up spies. My first sight of that deep grin had brought a click of vague familiarity—and then a jolt of recognition. It was like seeing a photograph of the jaunty Irishman I had grown up with, at long stretches off and on, wearing a snap-brim hat at a smart angle and grinning. Thinking he could get away with anything. And get away with it forever.

The memory was no longer painful or even embarrassing. *That was old Jack,* a friend of my father's had said. It explained everything.

Roxbury Parker's grin wasn't as self-assured. He wasn't an Irishman or a small-time, incorrigible criminal. The appearance of similarity vanished as soon as he spoke.

He pushed open the door to the Merrimack Inn. "You may as well register. I'll get us a table."

I got a key, dropped my second briefcase with the shirts and underwear in a small airy room with a four-poster and a view of the mountain. One corner of the room was filled with an armoire. The bathroom was recently renovated with blue tile.

I went downstairs and opened small-paned doors to a dining room. We were at the end of lunch and soon had the room to ourselves except for a waiter who said the catch of the day was gone. We ordered sandwiches.

"Have you and Axel Windlass known each other long?" I asked Parker.

"Twenty years, I suppose. He's down at the bank in Manchester, and I steer a fair amount of business to them. Bank trust departments are, huh, bank trust departments. Money dies of boredom rather than abuse. But Axel's people are pretty sharp."

"Had you done business with Mrs. Greenleaf for long?"

"Many years. Her husband left her well provided

for. It was almost eleven years ago that she moved up here." His thin voice had a whine of nostalgia.

"You were friends?"

"Oh, well . . . to be cynical about it, she brought me a good living, both on her own account and by recommending friends to me. Now a good third of my clientele live in Florida. But yes, we got on as friends. Saw eye to eye on ecology. Edna was quite a lady."

He smiled at empty space, as though he had had a crush on the widow.

"Does she have children?"

He came back to earth. "No. Except for minor bequests, Edna left her money to the Heuristic Society. I'm not too familiar with the group, but they underwrite scientific research. Edna had a lifelong belief in the importance of pure science. So, young man, what can you show me that the brokers in Boston can't?"

Without a whimper from my conscience, I fished out a prospectus for Puddyhole Exploration and explained why it would be rolling in cash when other oil companies had sunk their last hole. "The fellows running this are all veterans of multinationals," I said—leaving out pilferage, drinking problems, and whatever else had caused them to depart from the multinationals, "and they know how to ride the drilling cycle. They've been buying up foreclosed properties from the Houston banks that are desperate to get the bad loans off their books." I saw no need to mention that Puddyhole's chairman was the son of a Houston bank president.

Parker tapped a stubby tooth. "It all depends on the direction of hydrocarbon prices, doesn't it?"

"That's a shrewd observation. But if your costs are low enough, you can make money pumping even when oil prices are down."

Parker burrowed into the prospectus over lunch.

Given the pages he lingered over, I knew that the projections in millions of barrels and thousands of cubic feet were getting most of his attention. If you believed those numbers, the company was a bargain. He raised an eyebrow where Puddyhole had slipped another one past our due diligence people, laying out the imaginary barrels of reserves per $1,000 of debenture. If the numbers had been real, Roxbury Parker could double his clients' money in the debentures in two years. The damning stuff was in the back pages, and he didn't read that far.

He shrugged, pretending to be indifferent. "Mildly interesting, Mr. McCarry. I'm not much of a fan of energy investments, though. What else have you?"

We talked about Dairy Drive-Ins, and he said a pool he oversaw would be good for fifty thousand shares up to twelve dollars a share. We strolled down the street to his office. Where the mountain's shadow rested, the street was cool. Parker tucked his hands into his jacket pockets. "I suppose you will go away unhappy if I don't take some of that Puddyhole?" He grinned but didn't look at me.

"No, it's mostly sold," I said.

"Oh really."

"The yield plus capital-gain potential makes it popular." That failing, Mad Max would jam it into his children's college accounts. "But I wouldn't have brought it up if I didn't think I could get you some. The office manager and I have an understanding— best clients stand first in line. There's a block available if you want it."

His dingy eyebrows rose. "How much?"

"I'm pretty sure of five hundred units." That was a half-million-dollars' worth, leaving four and a half to go. I hesitated. "It would be difficult but there might be a way I can get you more."

"I could take a thousand. If you have something

71

that falls off the desk, a few thousand more . . . In return, you could take a half-point commission on the Dairy Drive-Ins."

"I'll have to work on it. Let's say, right now, that I can get you two thousand."

"Done."

Two thousand down. When I got back to New York I would call him with the good news that another three had showed up. Max would be my best friend for a day.

As I came out of the shower, there was a knock on the door. I hadn't ordered room service. I pulled on a shirt and linen trousers.

Robert Petrus scowled and grinned in one effort. "Hello, McCarry. Did you hook your fish?"

I thought about feeding him the towel. "Where's your boyfriend?"

"Knock it off. Greg and I just work together."

"I've never heard different. So where's Lord?"

"You don't need to know that." Same old Petrus. "Let me in."

I stood aside. "What are you doing here?"

"A just-in-the-neighborhood sort of thing. You don't think Greg trusts you to bring Parker in? You're only part of the picture."

"Not even a big part," I finished for him.

"I got curious about you," he said. He threw his narrow black attaché case onto the four-poster, glanced out at the scrubby mountain. He turned around and gave me his crackly grin. "It didn't take much digging. Your father was named Jack McCarry. Not a model citizen. He died in prison."

It had to be somewhere, I thought.

Petrus said, "Unjustly accused?"

Not unjustly. Inconveniently was closer to how Dad saw it.

He wrinkled his forehead. "Now I understand you.

That helps. You can't know how someone will jump unless you understand them. That's basic psychology. You're an open book."

"You're moving your lips."

"What?"

"Skip it. If I were you, this discovery would make me wonder whether McCarry could be trusted."

"I don't have to trust you. All I have to do is keep you on a short leash."

"Does Lord say you can do that?"

"A field operative's discretion. I'm using mine to yank your leash. Either you do what you're told and help this investigation, or the Treasury Department will charge you with obstructing."

"You'd never make it stick."

"So what? Your registration as a broker will be shot for moral turpitude. It won't matter how the charge plays out in court. So let's hear what Parker's up to."

"Buying stocks for the most part. Selling a few."

"What did you talk about? Stocks? The weather?"

"Edna Greenleaf. Mr. Parker gets misty on the subject."

"Guess who owns the mortuary where she was supposedly cremated?"

"Who?"

He snapped open his attaché case, sat on the bed with his black heels smudging the floor. "RPC Investment Partnership. As in Roxbury Parker Counsel. The partnership is registered in Manchester. From the looks, a lodgeful of M.D.s that Parker put together, mostly investing in real estate but with a few small companies. Whittier Mortuary is one of them."

He threw his notebook back into the case. The only other contents were a small calculator and a holstered revolver. If a taxpayer's audit came up wrong, Petrus could settle accounts on the spot. He raised his bony arm and inspected a watch. "You've got a car and can give me a lift."

73

"Use your own car."

"Greg dropped me off."

"Let Greg pick you up."

"I thought you wanted answers. Here's your chance. Besides, you're supposed to bend to my every whim, remember?"

We parked on the sloping shoulder of Route 7, at the crest of a valley. Across the road, a few country gentlewomen inspected hemlock trees and birdbaths at Pinchbeck's Nursery. Petrus pointed across a knobby hill to a broad driveway a hundred yards ahead. Between the trees stood a flat, sandy building with high chimneys. It looked like the light manufacturing plant that rural counties tolerate.

"Guess what that is?" Petrus said.

"Whittier Mortuary."

"That's right."

"Are we going to drop in?"

He shook his head. "You're going to wait here. I'm going to walk in a side door and look around before announcing myself officially."

I got out and leaned against the fender as he hiked along the thistly shoulder. An old woman picking through pansies watched me suspiciously. The key was still in the ignition, and the thought of abandoning him tried for my attention. If he managed to wring out a confession that Whittier hadn't really had a corpse named Greenleaf, he might forget about having to thumb a ride. If he failed to get a confession, he would be mean-minded whether or not I waited for him.

A rise in the ground obscured him for a moment. Then the bobbing head reappeared as he entered the parking lot and crossed to the north side of the building.

I waited. The old lady collected pansies. Sparrows chased each other along telephone wires.

After twenty minutes, three men came out the front door of the mortuary and got into a white Mercedes. It was almost five o'clock. Two other cars remained in the lot.

I lost track of the Mercedes as it passed behind a hummock. It emerged at the highway and headed north. I folded my arms and tried to look like I was waiting for Mathilda, to buy her pansies. The car whirred past.

A minute later another vehicle cleared out of the mortuary's lot. The day embalming shift was ending with no sign of my favorite Treasury agent. Petrus was enough of a gung ho jerk to hide in a casket until he could burgle the manager's desk. I pondered driving into the parking lot and leaning on the horn.

While I pondered, the Mercedes came roaring back. It had gone a quarter mile down the highway, out of sight, out of mind. When I heard the slide of tires and turned, two men in the front seat were grinning at me. It was number three, in the back, who swung a leg out. He had tight black curls, nut brown skin, a long face with a beard shadow. "Are you broken down, mon?"

"Just a little overheated."

"Yeah. It looks like you have trouble. Do you wanna lift to the Amoco?"

"No, it'll run okay once the engine cools."

"I don't see steam, you know? Perhaps it is okay now. My friend will advise you." The man next to the driver got out, a short black bull with a mustache that receded under his chin, iron biceps, plaited shoulder-length hair. He rolled past me and slapped a palm on the car's hood.

He reported, "She's cold, Rif. Anyway, I thought he stopped to pee."

Rif grinned, leaned on the door. "No, he stop to wait for Petrus. Hey—he want to talk to you, Petrus does, mon. He want you come to our office. Hey, do you work with Petrus for IRS?"

"No."

"You come here with him."

"We're double-dating a couple of local girls." I looked at my watch. "We're going to be late for smoked trout."

"Oh. Well, we give you a ride and you can remind Petrus. This is a courtesy on our part. We like to give you ride. As you can tell, I was not born in this country. My family would be offended if you declined to ride with me."

Dreadlocks was between me and my car. He was the part of Rif's family who would be offended.

A blond girl was at the reception desk, a brick horseshoe supporting racks of casket brochures. She was wedging files into a cardboard box. She worked fast. Her hand found something she didn't want, which she pitched onto the counter. It was a packet of lavender leaflets, *A Loving Alternative to Burial.* Papa could be freeze-dried or refried with equal love.

Rif leaned on the counter. "Is he still here?"

She didn't look up. "Go see for yourself. I've got to catch a plane."

"We go see Petrus," Rif announced. "What is your name, man?"

Petrus hadn't told him? "Lambrusco," I said.

"Come please."

I went. Whittier Mortuary was laid out more like an architect's suite than a place for morbid reflections on pissed-away years. Rif and Dreadlocks kept me between them as we crossed a wide arched doorway into a flowery viewing room. The casket was right up front. Either the family hadn't come or they had said all they could to Pops. Dreadlocks tapped his fingers on the coffin while Rif disappeared through a side door. He came back in a moment. "This way, Lambrusco. What your first name?"

"Cello."

He didn't get it. The side doorway led right to a prep room—a little awkward if a bereaved opened a wrong door looking for the bathroom and found the seamstress working on Aunt Betty's smile. The stainless-steel tables with scuppers like those on a fishing boat were empty. A tiled partition and windows separated us from another room. The wall facing us in that room had two features, a panel of dials and a bank of steel doors at waist height. A large man with a crew cut bent over a gurney rummaging through a black leather attaché case. He picked out a holstered revolver and a pocket calculator. The prep room was warm. Through the glass came a nearly imperceptible roar, like the firing up of a water heater.

The rummager changed position ever so slightly. My breath caught.

Bruno Mullins.

I turned a half step to smile at Dreadlocks and put my back to Mullins. Rif went into the next room to consult, leaving the door open. The water-heater roar was louder. Heat pushed in and surrounded us.

Dreadlocks cracked a mammoth grin. "Be hot in dere. Dat's de crematory."

I started to ask where Petrus was and didn't.

I trembled and supported myself on a utility table. There was a pan on the undercarriage that someone had left full of gizzards. With a choking sound I sank to one knee. When Dreadlocks bent down, I fed him the pan.

He recoiled as the slop hit.

As his eyes opened, he screamed and spat. I brought the pan around in a sidearm swing into his forehead.

When he tilted back, squealing, I dropped the pan and ran. I didn't look back. I had a twenty-foot head start on Rif.

At the front door, the lead was down to fifteen feet.

The blonde came around the desk to give chase. She stumbled as a heel collapsed. Rif leaped over her.

He was coming headlong, a little overbalanced, turning on the power to catch me a step beyond the entrance.

He would have, too, except that I closed the door in his face.

Only an aluminum hand bar kept him from coming all the way through the dappled glass. He leaned over the bar, bleeding onto the sidewalk, and tried to extricate himself by wriggling backward. The wreath of glass spears pointed outward, holding him like the flanges of a cat door. He tried straightening up and screamed.

I cut across the lawn, plowed through a scrim of brush. The highway was fifty yards ahead. All the time I expected to hear the roar of the white car. When I looked back, the car remained where Rif's buddy had left it. The blonde and Dreadlocks were at the entrance, dragging Rif inside.

Whittier Mortuary was being closed down fast. At the center of the building, a tiny ribbon of smoke leaked from a tall chimney and dissipated.

I wondered if Petrus had my name in his notebook. He was gung ho enough to have eaten the pages if he'd had time.

Rif and Dreadlocks had believed Lambrusco, but if Mullins found me in the notebook . . .

I started my car, swung from the shoulder straight across the dividing strip, and made fancy time back to the Merrimack Inn. It would take thirty seconds to pack, I told myself, and a minute to exchange my credit card receipt at the desk for cash. There were hotels around Logan, and for that matter Amtrak had a sleeper train from Boston to New York that had started to look attractive. Three Bloody Marys would get me home by morning.

12

I HADN'T COUNTED ON GREG LORD. HE WAS STRETCHED out on the four-poster, snoring lightly. I wondered what management thought of my visitors.

I kicked the bed. "Wake up, sweetheart! Bob Petrus won't be squeezing anyone else's balls."

He took the news without getting a handkerchief wet. In whatever corner of the Treasury they operated, one go-getter more or less was acceptable attrition.

"What will you tell his mother?" I asked.

"What will I tell his favorite sailor? Nothing. We've got a GS-12 who writes sympathy cards." He got up and collected his own black attaché case, pulled a revolver identical to Petrus's from a holster, and slid it into his pants pocket. "Did either of you learn anything?"

"I didn't."

"What about Roxbury Parker?"

"Front man. How many clients does he have?"

"Three that we've found. None worth more than a hundred grand."

Which left a wad unaccounted for. If I asked Lord how much money Parker controlled, he would have no reason to tell me. Instead I volunteered something. "Petrus had turned up a group of doctors who own Whittier Mortuary through Parker. He would need some legitimate business."

"I'm not arguing the point. I've just had a mail

cover going for two weeks, and Mr. Parker's client roster seems pretty inactive."

"He says he manages two hundred million," I tried.

"Does he?"

"It makes him just the kind of client I need."

"You should check his references."

"We had lunch today. I tried to imagine an old Yankee cleaning up money for the Boston mob. It didn't fit." It especially didn't fit with Bruno Mullins or his cosmopolite boss, Raab. But I didn't want to get into that. Bruno was my secret.

I fed him something to keep his mind occupied. "Mrs. Greenleaf's estate goes to something called the Heuristic Society. If your theory is right, it may be a front."

Lord shrugged. He had removed a one-column-wide newspaper clipping from his notebook and was studying it. He set the clipping on the bureau and went fishing in his blazer for a black cigar. "I didn't say anything about the Boston mob," he said.

"Who then?"

He rubbed a blunt hand holding the cigar across his face. "I can't tell you."

"Okay." I had wasted too much of my packing and leaving time.

He looked up. "I mean, I *can't* tell you. I don't know."

"That's okay."

He unwrapped the cigar. "We were trying a low-profile surveillance. I guess I can't blame Bob Petrus for screwing it up. From what you say they were closing down Whittier when you got there. Did you let anything slip to Roxbury Parker?"

"No."

"Then maybe it was the mail cover. Somehow they found out about it. If I were you, McCarry, I would be worried. Roxbury Parker must wonder how you happened to come up here at the same time as government snoopers. Might even suspect a connection."

"He may be sure of one. Some people at the mortuary got a good look at me."

"Go ahead and read that clipping. I left it there for you."

I went over and picked the paper off the bureau. The story was about four inches long, with a small headline, from the middle of an inside page. There was a note beneath the dateline: NYTimes Feb 8.

Brokerage Executive
In Fatal Plunge

Rudolf N. Marcade, a managing director of the government-bond department at R. D. Thomas & Stone, a securities company, died yesterday in a fall from a 33rd-floor apartment window on Fifth Avenue. He was 53 years old and lived in Manhattan, where he was prominent in cultural affairs.

The police have not determined the cause of Mr. Marcade's fall. The brokerage executive was inspecting an unoccupied apartment owned by a fellow employee. Mr. Marcade was scheduled to meet with a broker who was attempting to sell the apartment. . . .

I put the clipping down. "So what?"

"Marcade did business with one of the other people we're looking at."

"What other people?"

He didn't answer. I tried again, "Not Roxbury Parker?"

"Not Parker," he agreed. "Somebody like Parker, who does the same job Parker does, which is to scatter money around and make it look small and unimportant. Marcade helped him do that, invested in stocks, partnerships, annuities—all the things the little people do. Maybe he even knew Edna Greenleaf. From the article, I would guess he outlived his usefulness."

I felt a twitch in my cheek. "You're not going to panic me."

"I couldn't care less about panicking you. Our business, yours and mine, is done. Odds are you're blown, or at least that Parker would be too wary to let you get any closer. But I thought you deserved to know at least this much before I cut you loose."

"You haven't told me anything."

He shrugged. "The government's information is confidential. But you can look for answers yourself. Why would *you* act to obscure the origins of large amounts of money, McCarry? How many plausible reasons can you think of?"

"Apart from ties to organized crime?" I said.

"We don't think that's involved. Which lets out, for argument's sake, the standard stuff like drug profits, skim from Atlantic City, loan-sharking, mob-controlled businesses. How many possibilities are left?"

"Political slush funds?"

"Too much money."

"Latin American dictators?"

"They're accounted for."

I thought of Mullins—Swiss, hadn't Raab said? "Nazi treasure?"

"It's mostly safely reinvested in Bavaria. Well, that leaves the Russians. One of my superiors is convinced that the KGB is ready to buy General Motors."

"Let them. Car sales stink."

He shook his head. "Your funny streak won't get you far with Roxbury Parker's friends."

Talk of Parker's friends would have bothered me less if I knew who they were. Or how to extricate myself. I would tell Raab, *I was just passing through*

*New Hampshire yesterday, Herr Raab, and discovered
I have too many clients . . . ta-ta!*

I packed my briefcase slowly. Whether Petrus had
eaten his notebook didn't matter. Parker would be
comparing afternoons with his friends, and the question of visitors was bound to come up. All Parker had
to do was mention my name within Mullins's hearing
—or mention it to someone else who would mention
it to Mullins—and the coincidence would be too big
for Mullins's small brain to accept. Close questioning
of Rif or Dreadlocks would produce a description
uncannily familiar.

"Are you going to arrest Roxbury Parker?" I asked.

"What do you care?"

"He knows my name and description. If he suspects
me, I could be a clay pigeon for people I can't see."

He sat on the window side of the bed, smoking, and
peeked along the poor angle down to the street. "Your
name probably has already gotten around Parker's
circle. Have you landed any big accounts that weren't
normal referrals?"

Gustav Raab, Imrie de Wohl—they were knocking
the door down. Except that *I'd* chased Raab. Hadn't I?

"Nothing that stands out," I said.

"So I'm wrong. You've nothing to worry about. You
may as well hit the road." He didn't bother looking at
me.

"What about Parker? Why can't you arrest him?"

"There is a problem. The matter of a warrant. I
don't have one. Or tangible evidence. Or manpower.
There is only one of me, and his crowd is pretty
worked up. Between you and me, I would be satisfied
if I stood a good chance of getting out of town."

Eyes still on the street, he gestured with the cigar.
"Why don't you beat it?"

I almost twisted the knob, then turned back. "Draw
your own goddamned fire."

He chuckled. "All right, we'll leave together."

We set off along the hall, around to the back part of the floor. Lord hiked to the end of the corridor, where double doors opened onto a porch laid out with white wicker. He stepped outside. From the porch we had an unobstructed view of part of the village and hillsides where the sun was still strong. There was no stairway.

"Where is your car?" Lord said.

"Three streets over."

"We'll leave it. Nobody's seen mine and it's closer."

I leaned over the railing, scouting for Dreadlocks or other friendly faces. The brick patio below us, edged with slat-sided planters, was empty as the evening came along. Lord put down his case, climbed over the railing, and eased down until he was hanging from the floorboards. He swung for a moment and dropped to the patio. I tossed down our luggage and followed him.

A drinker in the dining room watched us with a restrained pissed-off expression.

We set off across the patio, ducked under an arbor, and headed down a graveled service road. The lane began at the inn's parking lot and arced past a pond where swans were honking themselves to sleep. After skirting the hotel grounds, the road entered a sparse woods. Buckled sections of iron fence cut us off on one side from weedy patches with a few headstones.

Lord was wrong about his car.

Two wheels on the grass, the blue four-door was nudged against the fence, passably nondescript except for the hood ornament.

Twice I looked at it. There was a loose sprawl of seersucker suit, bent knees, white socks, big shoes, bony wrists, long arms spread wide to hug the sky, flat-toothed grin, amber brows. Wire across the chest and around the wrists, a metal collar around the neck that seemed attached to a chain wound through the side windows.

Roxbury Parker's crinkled expression was hard to read. The eyes were as round as onions with blue sores in the middle. They rolled and saw me, and a tongue forced its way between locked teeth. He said, *"Heeeeee!"*

Licking his lips, he tried again and got a louder wheeze. *"Aaayyyy!"*

Lord didn't move. "Don't touch anything."

"It's Roxbury Parker," I said.

"Don't touch *anything*. Back away." He pulled his gun and watched the trees, tombstones, and car as if they would bite.

"Ahhhhhhhhhh!"

Lord pulled at my collar.

I stumbled after him thirty feet, looked back. Roxbury Parker's bent knee straightened as his heel slipped off the hood. His collapsing leg thumped the metal.

The sound that followed was much louder, a low heavy WHUMP! like gasoline exploding. A white flash enveloped the car. Roxbury Parker came at us, the part of him below the metal collar, riding the hood on a flat trajectory. A wave of hot air knocked me over. The car's roof and trunk lid turned cartwheels in different directions, trailing fire across the cemetery.

After a moment I raised my head.

Greg Lord sat in the ditch, clutching an arm. A silvery shaft, the mounting bar of a windshield wiper, protruded from the sleeve just above his elbow. Face slick, teeth set, he cursed softly as I separated the cloth. When I tore the jacket sleeve open, the blade fell against my hand. A deep gash parted his upper arm. Blood poured out in a lazy stream rather than a torrent.

He managed to look down. "My lucky day, I guess. Help me up."

I collected our bags. The car hood was on the roadside. I ignored it.

I looked around. No houses were near, and the fire had largely burned itself out.

"If we can find a phone," Lord said, "I can have someone take us out by noon tomorrow."

Until then we could camp in the cemetery. Instead, we covered a fast half mile down the lane, until the east side sprouted vegetable gardens and toolsheds. Near one of the sheds was a tiny Cape Cod with solar panels on the roof, a heat pump next to the woodpile, and an XKE parked under a tree. The house lights were off. "This is it," I said.

"Is there a key?"

I settled into a leather seat, pulled the ignition wires free. One of Pop's skills. We drove away without lights.

13

"YOU LOOK RESTED," MEG SORKIN SAID.

Having taken my turns driving all night, I recognized a diplomatic lie. At dawn, Greg Lord had sagged into a hotel bed and I had dropped by my loft for a shower and clean clothes. My face felt grainy. My stomach leaped and churned from six containers of truck-stop coffee. My brain yakked away at high speed without getting any words in order. I was barely alert enough to be suspicious of anyone paying compliments.

"Good morning, Meg."

If I could get past her into my office, I could take a nap.

"Lots of messages, Donald."

"Thank you." I headed for the door.

She bleated, "Timmy's leaving his wife!"

"That's a shame." I closed the door, ignored the stack of phone slips, and fell into my chair. The previous day had become a surreal video. If I closed my eyes, Roxbury Parker's sardonic grin sprang into focus. Behind him a sweltering room with a gas oven. Greg Lord's advice was irresistible. *Go home, tend to business as usual. You didn't see Roxbury Parker's corpse. Keep in touch.*

Pay your taxes.

Before the market opened, I dumped all five million worth of Puddyhole Exploration bonds into Edna Greenleaf's account. That earned me an A plus for scruples. I dug through the phone messages and returned calls that promised easy business. I gathered a couple of other orders, had Meg phone them down to the trading desk. Her voice was calm and efficient. I wondered if I had been hallucinating on the way in.

Bill Hinsdale had called again. And Patrick Squires. And all three Kimballs, within two hours of each other yesterday morning. Stacy, then Charlie, then Betsy.

Nothing from Herr Raab or Bruno.

I rang Bill and caught him just back from lunch. "Your client Rain Tree Capital is fancy merchandise," he said. "There was something about the name— almost familiar. I asked around. Gustav Raab comes from an old line of money managers. His uncle Friedrich was based in Paris before the war, Belgium before that, survived until the liberation. Friedrich and a brother, Samuel—that was Gustav's father— ran one of those quiet businesses where nobody is one hundred percent sure whether they're very exclusive or have trouble getting clients."

"I know the sort," I said.

"Gustav's father died back in the fifties or sixties, and the uncle retired about fifteen years ago. At least that's how my friend de Chabernay tells it."

"You're a sport."

"My pleasure. Thank you for the bourbon. Air express yet."

"Thank you for the stock."

"Don't grab your profit too quickly. Benjy's source says they have another contract coming."

We hung up, and I wished the Electronics Corporation of Belgium was in my own account instead of Rain Tree Capital's.

If Raab's pedigree was so respectable, why would he be tied up with Mullins? For that matter, Roxbury Parker had struck me as a solid, old-line Yankee. So unlikely to be working for Boston thugs that I had dismissed the idea. Not a totally wrong impulse. Rif, Dreadlocks, and Mullins were not Boston material.

Tax protesters.

I snorted, comfortably certain that you couldn't fool McCarry, not for more than six or eight months.

"Want to have some fun?" a high voice asked.

Isaiah Stern had opened the door without my noticing. He was tall and thin-boned, with a large cranium, a collar of limp brown hair, long fingers, hairy knuckles. His eyes shrank behind thick lenses.

"Fun," I repeated.

He wore a bold-striped shirt and patterned suspenders. "Just a few nickels worth," he said. "Join me in my office."

When Isaiah talked nickels, he meant five-hundred-share lots. Much of his fun was of borderline legality. Some of the best information in New York, he insisted, crossed over plates of gefilte fish at the Hillside Community Center. Half the younger generation had grown up to be corporate accountants.

Closing his office door, he said, "Have you heard of BF Corporation? Here's the annual report, but don't bother reading it." He sat at his terminal, tapped in a ticker symbol, BFB, and a column of numbers appeared. "They make office furniture, modular stuff, had a few bad years getting into automated production. The chairman controls about sixty percent of the two million shares. Other officers and directors have a bit. The stock available for trading is about six hundred thousand shares."

The green numbers flickered.

BFB 4¼ 2 12 3¾

4⅜ 5

4¼ 3

Without thinking, I translated. BF Corporation had traded two hundred shares this morning, all at $4.25 each. Someone—a tangible presence behind the ghostly green numbers on the screen—was offering to buy three hundred more at $4.25, and yet another somebody was willing to sell five hundred at $4.375. In the last twelve months, the stock had traded as high as $12, as low as $3.75.

"This is a company I wouldn't mind owning," Isaiah said reflectively. "The net worth is pretty solid at six dollars. There's about seven dollars a share in working capital. Bit of debt, of course, but rates are getting soft and they've been paying it down."

"You wouldn't have made money owning it this year," I pointed out.

"I've made a few nickels trading it. The price has been all over the place. It got up to eight dollars in May for no good reason. I got two points on the way up, then went short."

The phone rang. He flicked the speaker on. "Stern."

"It's Cheryl. You bought two hundred BFB at $4.25."

"Okay. Let's buy five hundred more up to three-eighths," he said and hung up. He explained to me, "I tried to get five hundred at a quarter, but the selling's run out. Now we'll goose it a little."

89

I sat on his leather sofa, locked my hands for a pillow. He got his stock a few minutes later at 4⅜. The screen then showed three hundred shares bid for at 4¼, one hundred shares offered for sale at 4⅜. Isaiah told Cheryl to buy five hundred up to 4⅜.

He was deliberately pushing the stock, trying to get the bid up without exposing himself too much to any big seller who might be hiding above the market. If there was a seller lurking, Isaiah would tempt him into showing himself on a few hundred shares rather than a few thousand. Ten minutes later, our trading desk had bought two hundred shares but hadn't filled the rest of the order. The screen showed BFB bid at 4⅜ for three hundred—that was Isaiah—with two hundred shares offered at 4½. He bought the stock at 4½, then bought another four hundred shares that showed up at the same price. He raised his bid to 4½. Nothing was offered at 4⅝ or 4¾, so the quote became 4½ bid, 4⅞ asked.

He swung around and gave me a triumphant grin.

"Anybody can run a thin stock," I objected. "Who will you sell it to?"

He had been waiting for the question, and the grin widened. "What I like about this thing, there's a chart reader over at Smith Barney. Every time this stock rises a point, he thinks he's seeing a breakout that will carry old BF back to twelve dollars. So he buys some for himself and calls all his clients to buy."

"How do you know all that?"

"Claire's niece works for this guy's partner. This is the second time this month that I've run this game on him. He'll fall for it again. You watch."

The green numbers flickered, and the price on the screen became 4⅝ bid, 4⅞ asked.

Isaiah crowed. "See! He's topped me. You can feel the difference. There's no stock around. All the sellers got out last week when it broke below 4. Now it's moving up, and a few people, like my weenie, are wondering if there's a reason. When the weenie starts gobbling, others will decide it's for real. They'll come in at 5½."

"If the weenie isn't on vacation," I said.

His eyes widened. "Don't say that! I should have checked. What's the matter with you, Isaiah?" He dialed an outside number from memory. When a young woman answered, he said, "Mr. Scheer's office, please. This is Fidelity Group calling. Is Mr. Scheer available?"

"He's on the other line," the girl said.

"I'll hold," Isaiah said and hung up. He punched Cheryl's number. "Let's buy two thousand BFB up to five." He leaned back and watched the action, chuckling when somebody invisible—the trader at Smith Barney or Mom or Pop in Des Moines—started moving to take stock away from him. "The weenie was on the phone to his dumb clients, telling them this is the big move. Or maybe I've hooked a day trader. Look at that—three thousand bought at 5⅛! You can hear him whispering to himself, 'BF hasn't been this strong in weeks—maybe there's a buyout.' These guys never learn."

I stood up. "Well, enjoy yourself. I've got to earn my keep."

"This show is nothing compared to what you missed yesterday," Isaiah said.

"What did I miss?"

"Timmy Upham's wife, Federica, stormed in here screaming what a no-good bastard her husband is. He hates her children. He betrays her with whores. He cheats her father on stock commissions. What could I do? I stood and watched."

"What did Timmy do?"

"He did nothing. He wasn't here. Federica was screaming at the walls, 'His cheap whore! His cheap whore!' "

"How did Meg take that?"

"Very well. She wasn't here either."

Isaiah waited for me to say "ahh" before he nodded. "The Sherwood Arms up the street still has its afternoon rates. Why not? The day drags a little, you hop up to the Spermwood to break the boredom. Me, I'm old-fashioned. I stay with one woman and watch the rest of you embarrass yourselves."

"Some of us have less control than others," I said.

"You should tell Timmy that his friend Isaiah wasn't the only person here for the spectacle. A remarkable thing happened. Our chairman, Thornton Wacker, chose the moment when Federica reached her crescendo to drop by. He seemed surprised to find so few brokers on duty. Only I, in fact."

"Where was Art?"

"Still at lunch. Unless they're sharing Meg. The bright side of this sorry incident is that Thornton Wacker doesn't know Federica Upham from a bag lady. If you came in on the middle of her rant and lacked the background, it wouldn't make any sense. Lucky Tim."

"Is he really leaving her?"

His brows rose. "This I hadn't heard."

When I passed the reception area, Meg avoided my eyes. I closed my door, checked, and found that BF Corporation had slipped back an eighth. Taking a guess at how long Isaiah would let the game run, I raised Cheryl and told her to sell short a thousand BFB at 5⅞, just in case it got there. She snickered. If she told Isaiah, my excuse would be that I was helping him knock it down for another play.

The game lacked its usual zest.

Charlie Kimball was at home. "Was your trip a success?" he asked.

I added Robert Petrus and Roxbury Parker together, subtracted a little something for their nuisance value, and said, "Not a complete waste. Have you talked to Greg?"

"No, I can't reach him. Look, I have to be in town this evening and thought we might have dinner. There would be no unexpected visitors from the government. You have my guarantee. Possibly two daughters, but they can be muzzled. Are you free?"

"Absolutely."

"Let me call you back with the time and place. Will you be there?"

"As long as I can keep my eyes open."

"Business is slow, then?" It wasn't what I meant. When I didn't correct him, he said, "If I had an account with you, would I have your full attention?"

I heard a bantering tone and responded. "My undivided attention. We could buy and sell your portfolio twice a day."

"How long would my capital last?"

"How much have you got? These things take time."

"You sound like a man tired of his chosen career, Donald."

"Too many Puddyholes," I said, not certain it was the reason.

"Oh, my God, yes! What a piece of work. Magee & Temple will have lawsuits coming at them from every direction, but I suppose they know that. You said you had a quota to fill. Have you done so?"

"Yes."

I must have imagined that the silence sounded disappointed. It bothered me. I said, "A deserving customer—I'll tell you about it at dinner."

"All right." He warmed a little, and I felt annoyed. What had he expected me to do, dump five thousand bonds off a bridge? He said, "You sound worn out. Perhaps you should get some sleep."

I gave him the number at the loft. He had never needed it before.

14

CHARLIE KIMBALL'S CHOICE OF DINNER SPOT SURPRISED me. The Portfolio Club had a meeting going on in the back room, which left us alone in the scuffed-up saloon.

Betsy was off primping when I arrived. Stacy kissed me demurely. I registered the essentials: that she smelled soapy, and seemed to be in good temper. Other details blurred, a blue flower-print skirt and a loose-fitting blouse, sandy hair pinned back, pale-green eyes distracted.

The sisters weren't alike. Betsy came back and gave me a resounding smack. She swept a glance around the wide plank floors and scarred tables. "Very authentic, Daddy. But where are the brass spittoons? Shouldn't there be somewhere for a gentleman to deposit his wad?"

Charlie looked to see if she was smiling.

"Classy question, dear," said Stacy.

Betsy turned to me. "Can you explain the oversight, Donald?"

"I don't think so."

"Daddy said you knew this place."

"I've been here once or twice. They've never had spittoons."

"There's some kind of meeting going on in the next room—a woman talking about alphas and betas."

"That's the Portfolio Club," Charlie said. "They meet here. I thought Donald would enjoy the familiar atmosphere. You're not a member, Donald? No, a born nonjoiner. But will you agree that they draw an interesting speaker now and then?"

I wondered if Stacy had told him about my pursuit of Raab. "The founder knows a lot of people," I agreed.

"Rick used to belong," Charlie told his daughters, who seemed to know who Rick was. "He used the contacts he made for job-hopping. I think he changed firms twice a year before settling at Nobscott."

A young man with a tall buzz cut came over and distributed menus. Betsy and her father ordered mixed drinks. I asked for a Samuel Adams, and Stacy went along. She leaned back and raised the menu, watching me from one half-hidden eye. She didn't know about Merrimack.

"Did Greg go back to Washington?" Charlie asked.

"I think he's still in town."

"And what can you tell us about your first sleuthing expedition?"

Charlie Kimball's input would have been welcome. But with his daughters present, the story would have gotten sidetracked, scrambled, and probably ridiculed. "It seems a pretty elaborate scheme," I said.

"And imaginative, I'll wager," Charlie said. "Evading taxes stirs men's creative spirit. It's a moral challenge for some people, resisting the lazy racial minorities' ascent, or the political hack's new public works project, or the dentist's daughter's student loan. You should see the tax shelters my brokers offer me. One woman was going to raise Shetland ponies in the Orkneys. Another had a four-to-one write-off on classical-record masters. The former was evading an arrest warrant on her last visit to this country."

The drinks came as raucous hee-hawing erupted from the back room. Pouring beer, I said, "You sound like you've converted to the anarchist church. Greg Lord would be offended."

He shrugged. His tan had a burnished red cast, as if he had been working on his rock wall. "Greg has no illusions about the average taxpayer. If the government couldn't employ intimidation, it wouldn't collect revenue. And if I didn't approve of the Treasury Department's efforts, I wouldn't have brought you and Greg together."

"Daddy probably cut a deal that we wouldn't be audited if he helped," Betsy said.

"We're audited every year, sweetheart. Both personal and corporate returns."

"They know better than to trust the Kimballs," she replied, having the last word.

Brokers drifted from the back room by twos and threes. Two-hundred-dollar shoes scuffed loudly. For a moment the room was taken over by a clumsy ballet of abrupt gestures, knowing grins and nods, heads tilted forward for special insights, smug laughs, pink faces, trim barbering. The choreography broke down as a few drifting men and women stranded themselves at the bar and others formed islands of chitchat. Faces I recognized bobbed into sight on the way to the door. Terrence Lippert emerged, tweedy despite the heat, pipe sticking from a breast pocket like a periscope, and bumped toward us. When I looked away deliberately, he came ahead. Stopping between Stacy and Betsy, he pushed back his long hair, stuck his chin out, and glanced casually down the front of Stacy's blouse. Attention divided, he said, "Hello, McCarry. I hope I'm not intruding. You'll be the first to see this."

A rolled copy of *Investor's Week* poked across the table. Charlie Kimball wrinkled his nose at the cover. I took the copy.

"The ink is still wet," Lippert said. "Your contribution is back there somewhere in my column."

I folded the magazine lengthwise and slid it into my jacket. "Thank you, Terrence. I'll read it tomorrow."

He nodded at the brush-off but remained, hands in

his pockets. I said, "Is your profile of Raab in this issue?"

"He's still not cooperating. In fact, he seems to be closing doors before I get there." His voice was peevish, as if putting him off were unfair. His pale knobby face was almost forlorn. "Raab's friends won't talk, and his brokers don't take my calls. I can't get close to Raab himself because the secretary has learned my voice. And he's got that thug answering the door. The bastard's with him here tonight."

"Too bad," I said—and looked at the menu.

"You didn't make any headway with Raab?"

"He runs a closed shop," I said.

Stacy leaned around and looked up at Lippert with a mischievous smile. Her intention was transparent. *Donald has certainly been banging on the door.* She saw my expression and settled back into her seat, laughing.

I began reading the menu with full attention. Charlie asked his daughters what they were having. Terrence wanted to hang around waiting for Stacy to reach for her drink. But nobody said anything, and he murmured something to himself and left.

When he was out of earshot, Stacy leaned forward. "Why didn't you set him up with your prize catch, Donald? He wouldn't give away your deep knowledge of foreign markets."

"Some clients value discretion."

"He's kind of a pathetic character," she said.

If we'd been alone, or at least without Charlie, I'd have asked why she let him make such a leisurely inspection of her breasts. Thinking of Betsy, I shrugged.

Lucius Astenberg wheeled out of the back room, guided by a blond man with muscles on his forehead. My viscera melted, and the taste of beer rose in my throat. Bruno Mullins scanned the room, ignoring orders shrilled by the onion-headed creature in the

97

chair. Astenberg craned around, tugging at his driver's sleeve, features pinched like crumpled paper, spittle glistening on his chin. Behind Mullins, like a burgher tending to an unpredictable guard dog, Gustav Raab appeared and drew Mullins's attention to duty. Raab bent closer to Astenberg's desiccated lips, nodded. Mullins's eye followed as a scarecrow arm jabbed at a spot across the room.

Directly at—

All three fell on us.

Charlie Kimball got out of his chair to shake the trembling hand. "Lucius, still as civil as ever, I see."

"Still suffering the company of damned fools." A gobbet of spit arced across the table. Betsy leaned deftly out of the trajectory. Astenberg sprayed, "Our speaker tonight believes that the markets are essentially efficient—and therefore rational—and therefore invulnerable to useful analysis. In a word, that they cannot be *beaten!* How does she explain my wealth, Kimball?"

"You are a random deviation from the norm," Charlie said.

"Ah-hee!"

Bruno Mullins straightened, folding his arms across his chest, and stared through everyone. He paid me no more notice than the rest of the room. Standing, I exchanged nods with Raab, reached across to shake his hand. He smiled at the sisters. "My dear boy, I did not expect to see you here this evening."

"It's a surprise to me as well." I did the introductions, neglecting Mullins.

"Such lovely young ladies," Raab said. The Old World charm was thick as jam. "I am loathing to discuss commerce in the presence of beauty." He tilted his head and almost winked, voice going falsetto. "Still, one must!"

"Go right ahead," Betsy said. "Daddy bores us all the time."

He giggled. "If I had known we would meet, Donald, I would have pried you away from your friends during the program. What delightful action in Electronics Corporation of Belgium! Did you see this afternoon's close?"

"Fifty-two."

"Up seventy percent in two months! Just splendid! The portfolio is performing extraordinarily well for so short a time."

"Luck and a strong market help," I said.

"But so does skill. Do not underrate yourself, young man. You have the makings of a superior money manager."

"Thank you. Coming from you, that's quite a compliment."

"There is a bit more money I would like you to handle. I am going abroad, so we should discuss it soon." He made a fussy, annoyed gesture that didn't tell me anything. "One must keep clients happy. I am telling you nothing you do not know, yes? Besides investing the capital wisely, one must cultivate the client personally. And that means an occasional dreary week of travel."

He looked as implausible as he sounded, the bottom-heavy duckpin pouting above his goatee over a junket. However attentively Raab stroked and soothed his clients, he would work them around visits to first class restaurants.

Lucius Astenberg had run out of libels to heap on dead enemies. Perhaps the names were drying up in the old skull like dust sifting off ancient shelves. He made an empty sucking noise.

Charlie and Raab exchanged courtesies, and wringing her hands, Betsy interjected, "Mr. Raab hates the thought of going abroad! How could I survive such an ordeal?"

"A pretty lady should suffer Paris if she wishes," Raab said. He shrugged at me. "I wish you and I had spoken earlier, Donald. Your assistance on this trip would be appreciated. It is difficult to convince many of our investors that the United States market is not mad."

"Hard to convince me of that," Lucius spat.

Raab ignored him. "You would be a great help, Donald. You are well-spoken, you have a professional's perspective, and you are more presentable to gentle people than Bruno. I do not suppose—no, it is too much to ask. You have other clients. And even if you felt you could remove yourself from the office for—a week, let us say?—you would not want to be separated for so long from a lovely friend." His eye traveled unerringly to Stacy. He gave her a Kewpie-doll grin. "You would not be planning a vacation, my dear?"

I tried semaphore-fast blinking to get her attention.

Stacy grinned back at him. "I'm always planning a vacation. A week?"

"A day more or less. It depends on how our meetings can be arranged. Perhaps you could help us prepare them. It is rather tedious work—"

"Wait a minute," I said. "It's generous of you—"

"Not generous at all! I will drive the lady very hard. There will hardly be more than three-quarters of each day free for shopping, or the Tuileries, or whatever lovers do in Paris this summer."

"The gallery can spare me," Stacy said. "Can't your clients spare you, Donald?"

Very easily, I thought. Raab saw Betsy sulking and an instant later had hired her for the entourage. He deferred to Charlie as an afterthought. "Only with your permission, of course?"

Lucius Astenberg found more spit. "Go ahead, Kimball. The girls are safe with Gus. Look at this hulk he's got guarding him." He craned around to show his teeth to Mullins.

Charlie said, "I'm sorry to be a wet blanket, but I

was planning a little excursion of our own. Sorry, Mr. Raab."

"What excursion?" Betsy demanded. "You just don't want us off raising hell."

Raab folded his fingers like a bishop expressing regret. "And you, Donald?"

"I think I can make it."

He sent Mullins out for the car and steered Lucius over near the door to wait. They seemed to have run out of conversation. I watched them ignoring each other while Stacy and Betsy heaped guilt on their father. They'd had years of practice.

After dinner was soon enough to hatch a plan for sinking my part of the junket before it set sail. On no account would I share close quarters with Raab's bodyguard.

"How did you ever meet such a nasty old man?" Betsy asked her father. She mimicked through a wet tongue, "My name is *Luschioush Ashtenberg.*"

"Lucius is semiretired nowadays, but for quite a few years he managed part of Tracer Minerals' profit-sharing plan."

"How did he do?" I asked.

"Modestly better than the market. One and a half or two percent better a year. He was extremely consistent."

Betsy sniffed. "Pretty pathetic, I'd say."

Charlie gave her a glance like a pat on the hand. "That statement reveals how little attention you've paid to me for seventeen years. Small advantages add up, Elizabeth. The difference between a consistent return of six percent and one of eleven percent may be the difference between no fortune and a quite sizable one. You might need six percent to live on. The extra five percent represents real growth of capital." He uttered the word "capital" with reverence. Not quite as hushed as a prelate invoking the hereafter but like a poet caressing "truth" and "beauty."

His daughter straightened. "What does five percent add up to?"

"It depends on how long it compounds. If you had bought a thousand dollars worth of Napoleon's bonds around eighteen hundred, the five-percent yield would have given you about thirty million by now."

In a pale linen suit, with her hair tied up, she looked younger than seventeen. "Is Daddy pulling my leg?" she asked me.

"No."

Charlie smiled. "If Napoleon raised ten million dollars, that one bond issue would be worth three hundred billion today. If he had kept paying."

"So why didn't that happen?"

"It never happens. It can't. The old stories—defaults, taxation, confiscations—all interrupt the compounding. The process of compounding is so ferocious that it *must* be interrupted. Last year, your mother's trust earned twelve percent. At that rate, it takes six years for the principal to double. Six more years for it to double again. What's the logical inference?"

She shook her head.

He looked at me.

"As interest rates rise, people inevitably break their promise to pay," I said.

Charlie nodded approval. "And that, my dear, is why we have sold some of the bonds from your mother's trust. The companies just can't keep paying at these rates. Nobody can hand over twelve percent annually without trying to take some of it back by reneging."

We had dinner, and Charlie complained he had an early morning. He and Betsy left for a hotel. Stacy and I walked two blocks to an avenue and got a taxi to SoHo. In the fluttering light from the street, I skimmed *Investor's Week* looking for Terrence Lippert's column. It was in the back, decorated by a sketch of a limp oil derrick. He had devoted most of the page to tearing apart the financial condition of Puddyhole Exploration. I couldn't make out the numbers, but he seemed to have cataloged every sin.

Drowsily I settled back. If *Investor's Week* made it onto New York's main newsstands tonight, Puddyhole's price tomorrow morning would look like a bucket of bricks heading down a well. Magee & Temple's bond sale would die ingloriously. Even if our clients weren't sharp enough to revoke their purchases —or to renege on paying—the venerable firm of Magee & Temple would rise from its stupor, exhale loudly, and mumble about withdrawing the offering until market conditions improved. Which for Puddyhole would be when oil topped fifty dollars a barrel, not before. With oil under twenty, bankruptcy seemed a more immediate prospect for the company.

Having sunk a profitable piece of business for my employer—and more than likely sunk its client— should have filled me with shame. Or at least aroused a twinge of remorse. Instead I felt smugly, tiredly content. A few thousand of our customers would be richer. Mad Max would tear up his quotas. Thorny Wacker would bail out a different bunch of Texans.

"Is that an article on the stock you've been complaining about?" Stacy asked.

"A bond, actually—debt instead of equity."

"What difference does it make?"

"Not much, darling. They're both worthless." I yawned. "We had a chance of selling the bonds because they were supposed to pay sixteen percent annually. If our customers just looked at the promised yield, not bothering to inspect the worthless collateral, we were home free."

"Sixteen percent of nothing is still nothing," she objected.

"Sooner or later it would be, when Puddyhole missed an interest payment. Until then, we would cash the customers' checks and hope they forgot where they bought the bonds."

"And if they remembered?"

"'Magee & Temple is graciously accepting new clients,'" I said.

On the street outside my building, a storefront theater and neighborhood restaurants were still trading customers. I paid the cab. In the elevator, Stacy wrested *Investor's Week* from my pocket and skimmed Lippert's column. She delivered her verdict. "I know it's not my subject, dear, but this sounds nasty."

I nodded. "If he has the numbers right, that's all that's necessary."

"Did you give him the numbers?"

"Yes."

The elevator bumped to a halt. My consciousness had sunk to zombie level, shot through with hideous images from Merrimack. It was thirty hours since Roxbury Parker had cartwheeled headless over the village lane.

I fingered my key to open the door to my loft. Stacy blocked the latch. "Donald, isn't that risky?"

Memory of the last minute had fled. "Isn't *what* risky?"

"Isn't it risky to tip a reporter about your firm's deals?" Her eyes were wide and bright, her smile luscious. I knew I had missed something. She pressed on. "Wouldn't Magee & Temple fire you if they knew?"

"If they knew."

"But you gave that man the numbers anyway, because the deal was so dishonest." She wrapped arms around my neck. "You're not as cynical as you pretend."

There was no point in telling her that Lippert would never have heard from me if Max hadn't gotten pushy with his quotas. Celebrating my integrity might be the only thing that could keep me awake another half hour.

I unlocked the door.

It was an awkward moment.

Timmy Upham scrambled off the couch, suspenders askew. I glanced around but saw no sign of Meg Sorkin. Timmy winced. "Sorry, folks. I probably shouldn't have come here."

"Who is this?" Stacy asked.

"He works with me."

"I shouldn't have come here, but Federica kicked me out," he said, more in Stacy's direction. "So I had a few drinks and needed someone to talk to. Your keys, Don, everybody knows about the set in your desk."

Stacy patted my shoulder. "You boys stay up and talk. I'm going to bed."

The sleeping area was screened from the rest of the loft by chest-high bookshelves and an armoire. She disappeared, and after a rustle of clothes, the bed creaked invitingly. I glared at Timmy.

He smiled vaguely. "This was really a bad idea. I know it. I shouldn't try to figure things out with martinis."

"Why didn't you figure them out with Meg in her apartment?"

"She wants to cool it a little. If Max finds out, she's afraid of losing her job."

"I thought Thorny Wacker had found out. Doesn't he talk to Max?"

Shrugging, Timmy sagged back onto the couch. Not the reaction I wanted. Timmy mumbled, "I don't think old Wacker-off knew what Federica's fuss was about. What really got Meg worried was, is, I was talking about leaving Federica. I'm sure of what I want, Don. This is altogether serious."

"Good."

"She's nervous, though, about a serious commitment."

I nodded.

"She's worried about kids," he said. "I've made that clear. I'm basically a family guy. I want Meg to have my kids. *Our* kids. And she'll get along with Bunny and Sarah like their own mother."

I didn't want to encourage him, so I didn't say anything.

He rambled on. "It's a lot for Meg to absorb all at once. That's the problem. But I've been head over heels in love with her since our first afternoon together. That was *special.*" He smiled at the memory.

"That's just great," I said.

"The two of us, trying everything like it was all new. All that gentle touching . . ."

"Fine, fine." If Meg ran away, we would be without a secretary again. And if Federica dumped him for good, Timmy could end up sleeping on a park bench, unless he thought he had dibs on my couch. I asked, "Do you want a cup of coffee?"

"No. I guess I'm awake. I'll get a room at the Gramercy."

"I'll call a cab."

"Don't bother. I can use a walk. There'll be cabs up on West Broadway."

I let him out and went back to see if Stacy was awake.

15

Max Oberfeld showed up just before noon. He came off the elevator with spidery hands tucked into his pants, blue coattails flapping, and pretended to saunter into the suite. The froggy eyes roamed restlessly, knowing that somebody had peed in the pond.

At Meg's desk he scanned the closed doors. "Good morning, Miss Sorkin."

She was working on expenses for my New Hampshire trip. Deftly, the account disappeared. "Good morning, Max."

"How are your charges?"

"Behaving themselves."

"Say—by chance do any of your boyfriends talk to a chap named Lippert?" He sounded especially friendly.

"Named Lipper?"

"Lippert."

"Lippert? Not that I can think of."

"Doesn't matter." He smiled. "Anybody getting interviewed these days?"

"Interviewed?"

"By the press, sweet. They call brokers looking for ideas. Though why they would call any of these four I can't imagine."

"I think you're right, Mr. Oberfeld. Our guys don't get many calls from reporters."

He looked away from her and caught me watching from the news wire. I waved. "Hi, Max."

He came over. "You've placed all your Puddyhole, haven't you?"

"I took your suggestion and added it to the Greenleaf account. Income for the heirs."

"And Upham?"

"I don't know. He had a client meeting this morning."

"Bradshaw?"

"Got the flu."

Max pivoted, bumped into Isaiah, who pulled a Styrofoam lunch platter out of jeopardy as Max stalked to the elevator.

"They haven't opened Puddyhole, have they?" Isaiah whispered.

"Apparently not."

"Had you sold yours?"

"To a dead woman."

"They never kick, do they?"

My lunch date had been scheduled for more than a week and couldn't be ducked. Carole Hale ran a small money-management firm called Contrary Investors and played brokers off like schoolboys wanting a feel. She had been teasing me for more than six months with hints of bringing more of her business to Magee & Temple.

Over clams casino she launched into the failures of her favorite brokers. George Hermano of Providence had been feeding her bad takeover stories since spring. "He would have to get the word on a half-dozen deals just to get me even," Carole said. Her short blond bangs quivered. "And then the Securities and Exchange Commission would be on my case. Where are they when I'm hearing lousy tips? They never come and say, 'Poor Carole, we'll get your clients' money back.' And the mess Hermano has made is only half my problem. This fellow at Pru got me into two hundred thousand shares of Nu-West

Industries just before fertilizer prices collapsed. Can you believe that? I feel like Typhoid Mary, except instead of making people sick I attract losers wherever I go."

"Life's tough," I agreed. "Did you buy any Tiger like I told you to?"

"Do I really need to add to my woes?"

"If Pacific trade holds up, Tiger will make a lot of money and you will look very smart."

"If I buy any Tiger, I'll put the trades through you. But I'm not a believer yet."

"All right."

"What are they going to earn?"

"Two bucks. The stock is ten."

Lunch arrived, twenty-dollar entrées because the waiter captain remembers customers' names. Carole stabbed at poached swordfish, mentally working the money she might make on Tiger if the stock ever sold at seven times earnings. She pushed around a parsleyed potato.

"What have you got that's not so risky? Something with good dividend income. Weren't you boys doing an oil company debenture?"

"That may be withdrawn," I said.

"Is it too good to share with the public?"

"Not exactly."

"You don't deny that your firm's partners keep the best deals for themselves?"

"I couldn't deny that if I wanted to," I said. The good ones never got shown around on our floor, so I couldn't deny what I didn't know about. But in principle, Carole was right. If a bit of business looked attractive, Magee & Temple's partners would try to swing it as a private deal. They would reserve pieces for the upper echelon at the firm and for friends selected for financial, social, or political connections. If a bit of business looked so-so, it might be set up so that senior drudges like Max Oberfeld could buy in before the public. If the package fell short of being so-so, a platoon of brokers was ordered out of the trenches.

Carole Hale wagged a finger across the table. "If you don't get me a piece of the sugary deals, I shouldn't give you my other business."

I walked back up Broad Street to the office and joined Isaiah Stern in his cubbyhole watching Puddyhole get pounded. The specialist on the floor of the stock exchange had found enough buy orders by twelve-thirty to absorb the early selling. He had opened trading at 4¼, down 1½ points from the previous afternoon's price. An hour and a half later, Puddyhole was 3⅜ and sinking. As each wave of selling hit, the price submerged, bobbed feebly, and wallowed. It was like watching a drowner getting weaker.

"It would have been a beautiful short sale if we had known," Isaiah said.

"The trading desk would have turned you in to Max."

"Everyone down there loathes him. He's always sticking them for tickets he says they lost. I could still get a thousand off short. This stock has death written on it."

No sooner had he spoken than two bashings knocked Puddyhole down to 2⅞. Isaiah sighed and decided it was too low to sell short.

16

I TOOK A CAB TO THE EDGE OF SoHo AND WALKED OVER TO Spring Street. My evening looked vacant. Stacy had left the gallery at noon and her apartment hadn't answered at four-thirty.

The neighborhood cafés were crowded with an odd mix of artsy-fartsies and Wall Streeters. Six years into a bull market, everybody who couldn't get a job with his brother-in-law was an investment banker in training. After two months they were all deal makers, baby-bottom-smooth cheeks puffed out around expensive cigars, red suspenders holding up pleated pants from Barney's. I elbowed my way through a blabber of mergers, leveraged buyouts, discounted cash flows, currency adjustments, bond defaults, not-to-worrys—and only noticed when I reached the bar that half the yakety-yak was coming from guys and girls with Mohawk haircuts and blue eyebrows. The artists were wondering if they could hike the royalty rates for the limited-edition serigraphs that Ms. Mary was scattering up and down Manhattan and to all points west. If they made a few more bucks, they could scarf up some zeros and retire to Bhutan in a few years.

Sipping an ale, I scanned the afternoon tabloid for a word or two about a ghastly decapitation-bombing incident in New Hampshire. Roxbury Parker had been squeezed out by New Yorkers' chauvinistic preference for our own bizarre mayhem. I was halfway through something of the dog-saves-burglar-by-eating-tot variety when my elbow got jostled. The lady who had bumped me had round Asian cheeks, a delicate nose, amber eyes, and a pout. The pout I noticed first because I expected it to apologize. She looked down and decided my elbow was at fault.

I was noticing other pieces, not sure how they fitted together. Her skin was like a poor grade of opal, milky white without the subdermal glints of green and pink that dress up a stone. She wore loose-fitting black pants tucked into ankle boots, a black turtleneck, teardrop garnet earrings.

"It's your turn to buy," she said.

Did I say she didn't know how to apologize? She specified Campari and orange juice. The English was quirky, with a stretch to the vowels that could have originated in Italy or Greece or almost anywhere else.

"This is ridiculous," she confided. "I saw you come in and decided to pick you up."

"That's not ridiculous." Despite the bar's air-conditioning, my neck was suddenly wet.

"It is, because I don't know how to do it. I edit travel guides. This is a departure." She pouted. "I don't actually get to *edit* them. I just make sure names are spelled right and there are enough commas."

The drink came, and she lifted it. "Cheers, and thanks for the drink. My name is Jerry, with a *J*. I don't pick guys up very often, even cute ones. You never know who's got the plague. But you look substantial and safe. Can I guess what you do? You're a banker."

"Not bad, a stockbroker."

"I was close. You know, now that I've picked you up we could go somewhere. Like up to Sixty-second Street."

"What's on Sixty-second Street?"

"My flat. You haven't got another date, have you?"

"No."

"Then why are you still sitting here?"

"I don't believe in manna from heaven. When it falls into my lap, I get suspicious."

"You're a pessimist. Sometimes a good-looking guy just gets lucky. Besides, I'm not in your lap yet." She tucked her tongue into the Campari and drank like a hummingbird.

We would scurry uptown, McCarry panting. Then somewhere the little creature would introduce me to her big bad friend from Merrimack.

I was getting paranoid.

She read my thoughts. "Gee, if you lived around here we could save a trip. The only problem is, there's a boyfriend—ex, very ex—who hangs around SoHo. Higgy is kinda nuts."

"What does Higgy do for a living?"

"Some kind of consulting—I don't know, and what do you care?"

"I live just up the street," I said. "We could probably make it without being spotted."

She chose to misunderstand. "Having someone watch is half the fun." Sliding off the stool, she tugged my arm. "Come on anyway. You can take charge till we get to the good stuff."

She wasn't big enough to be dangerous by herself. I could keep an eye on the street for trouble. If her pal Higgy resembled Bruno Mullins or one of his chums, it was time to leave town. Old Jackie McCarry taught cutting a losing game. His son had taken the lesson.

A little panther arm tugged, and I went.

Once past the door of my building, I felt safe. Unless Timmy Upham had been selling my keys on the street corner, I wouldn't meet anyone I hadn't invited. The bottom two floors of the building housed a flower shop and a mail-order garden-seed company, but they had a separate entrance. My residential neighbors were a photographer, a shoe importer, and a young couple who traveled most of the time. All were longtimers. All believed in minding their own business and keeping the world at bay. They had installed the locks and security system before I arrived. The front door, the elevator, and the interior doors were all controlled by skate-key locks. Everyone used the same keys for the front door and the elevator, but it took a separate key to get the elevator door to open at each loft. Mine was on the fourth floor.

"You're acting spooky," Jerry said leaning against me. "I hope you don't turn out to be a weirdo."

"I hope not," I agreed.

She hadn't bothered to ask my name.

Maybe it didn't matter for a short acquaintance.

She wrapped an arm around my neck, stretching taut. Under the loose clothing she seemed to be all rubbery springs, more a dancer's body than a comma checker's. She reached a toe out and hooked the back of my knee, pulled firmly. The amber eyes stared with more hunger than I usually inspired. "Baby, you promise to give Jerry a workout."

"Not in the elevator."

"Pooh."

We jerked to a stop and I opened the door. She strode into the living room, where the light was receding. I stayed with my back to the elevator. As the door slid shut, the lock engaged with a soft chunk.

"You've got a pretty nice place. Would you offer me a drink?" She scouted out the expanse on silent feet. If she'd had a tail, it would have been standing straight up. If she'd been a little male panther instead of a female, the couch and stereo rack would have gotten squirts of urine.

She stopped in the arch to the kitchen. "About a drink?"

"In the cabinet next to the books. Help yourself. There's ice in the refrigerator."

"Most guys who've been as lucky as you would mix

me one." Squatting, she dug through the liquor cache and settled on a bottle of sour mash. She disappeared into the kitchen. "I'll make you one too."

I hadn't moved from the door. Apart from her prowling, which barely raised carpet dust, the loft was silent. I could see into most of the corners but not every hidey-hole. The door had been locked. It was locked now. I decided to trust my locks.

I dropped my keys into a jacket pocket, threw the jacket onto a chair. Clever fellow. She would never get loose. All the black-hatted letches on television used to swallow the keys. My old man watched the cartoons with me and pronounced the tactic dumb. "Some women you gotta run from without taking a shit first."

She inched out of the kitchen, holding a tumbler in each hand. She sipped from one drink and raised a toe in a faint kick. "I do it right, if I do say so. Here, come get yours. A little water and a little ice."

I walked over and took the drink. Twenty-dollar bourbon needed neither water nor ice. I was polite. "Very nice. Now down to business. Why don't you tell me who told you to pick me up?"

"Wow, a paranoid. How about a little fun first? Action first, talk later." Her eyes were dreamy in a way that prickled my neck hairs. The chemical of Jerry's choice wasn't bourbon. Sipping the drink, she scrunched her feet together and worked off first one black cloth boot, then the other. Her toes were white and strong-looking. She handed me the glass. "Baby, hold this."

She bent and slid down the baggy pants, kicked them free and stood with her heels together in a dancer's pose. Her calves and thighs were sheathed in smooth white flesh that softened the lines of powerful muscles. A tremor of tension passed through her from her toes to as high as I could see, which was just above a deep teardrop navel. The mons was plump and bare

115

except for a dusting of black stubble. Yasser Arafat's chin, I thought, trying to remember if the little killer had a cleft.

"Now Jerry gets her workout." She bent a knee, raised her right foot slowly to my hand holding her glass. She brought her toes up under the glass. Her balance was perfect. I opened my hand and the tumbler settled onto manicured toes. She smiled roundly. "Watch this!"

On her left toes she pivoted in a full circle, balancing the glass. Not quite the Rose Adagio but interesting. When she faced me again, she raised the foot. "Have a sip."

As I bent forward she giggled and lowered the glass. "Try again."

I reached lower. Then she moved very fast. I was still bowing to follow her toes when the tumbler catapulted away and the knee sailed into my forehead. A heel came from somewhere—she must have been pivoting again—and numbed my cheek. I landed on my side six feet away and looked around for my head.

She stood motionless, humming something. Coming out of her concentration, she noticed me. "Baby, *please* get up."

I started to, and her nimble toes flung an empty tumbler at me. It was leaded crystal. I ducked.

"Up, up!" she commanded.

I scrambled behind the sofa and heard panther feet moving across the floor. The panther brought in a friendly buffalo that came out of nowhere and stomped between my shoulder blades.

Then she was ten feet in front of me, staring down critically. "You aren't going to last long."

She turned away and thumbed through a few records next to the stereo rack. She slid a disc out. "Who's Martha Argerich? Is this a rock group— Schumann? Never mind. I'm *bored.* Higgy said it would be like this. But I hoped you would put up a fight, baby."

She came at me again but didn't really try to land a blow. As I stumbled to my feet, she flickered across the fading light in the east windows. The black turtleneck was almost lost in the room's dimness.

Edging toward the elevator, I wished I hadn't gotten so cute with the key. Or that I kept a meat cleaver lying handy. She cut me off with a kick that numbed a shoulder and would have snapped a neck.

When I lurched for the kitchen, she danced around and blocked the arch. Waving her hands, she cooed, "Come to Jerry."

I backed away, bumped a chair and heard the soft pad of bare feet. She bounced on the cushions of the couch with both feet and somersaulted off, head tucked, hair flying. Thighs slapped my cheeks and we went backward hard. When my eyes opened, she was sitting far forward on my chest, elbows resting on her knees. She was breathing just hard enough that her belly button shivered. Her left thigh bore a tattoo of a lady's face with red snakes for hair.

"Baby," she whispered, tousling my hair, "if you have a really fancy tongue I might forget what I'm doing."

I heard the elevator door open. Her friends had come to see that she didn't forget. A chagrined voice cried, "Oh shit! I didn't know you were here."

I tilted my head, collecting a case of whisker burn, and saw Timmy Upham with Meg Sorkin beside him. They gaped at Jerry. Timmy fought against a grin. "I didn't mean to barge in."

Jerry came off me and I mumbled a warning. She headed straight for Timmy, who was frozen in choked giggles. Jerry kicked the center of his chest, knocking him against the door frame. He gasped. He clutched his chest and pitched forward. The girl chopped a flat hand at Meg's neck. Meg was already twisting away. Grabbing her hair, Jerry tried a kick at the exposed neck. She missed, overbalanced, and pulled Meg down.

Jerry got free first, nose spilling blood. I hit her in the muscled back as hard as I could, ducked away as she spun. The rubbery legs wobbled. She held a hand to her nose. Blood trickled over her knuckles. Breathing between tiny teeth, eyes glazed, she stumbled back into the elevator. We stared at each other until the door closed.

Timmy Upham retched loudly, and Meg held him. He wiped his mouth. When he could talk, he said, "How long have you been seeing *her?*"

"Just today."

He rubbed his chest. "Nice girl. Let me guess, you made a pass and she defended herself."

"That's about it."

"But not quite the truth," Meg Sorkin said. She helped Timmy to his feet and he sagged comfortably against her.

"It's close enough." I had never gotten much idea what Meg thought of me. Her polite nod said it wasn't surprising that McCarry had weird friends.

Timmy wheezed for her sympathy. For me he managed an embarrassed grin. "We tried ringing here fifteen minutes ago. There was no answer, so I figured you were off with that Kimball girl."

"So you thought you would use my place again. How long has this been going on?"

"Just this once," Meg said. "Honestly."

"We're stuck," Timmy explained. "Meg has a roommate who's pretty religious."

"Why not use a hotel?"

He said sheepishly, "Federica canceled my credit cards."

When he felt mobile, I helped him over to the kitchen bar. I started a pot of coffee, turned on lights, and went back through the place looking for damage. There was surprisingly little. The two heavy tumblers had landed on the carpet and survived. Her shoes and pants lay between the kitchen and the couch. I rolled them into a ball, couldn't think what to do with it and tossed it back onto the floor.

I poured Timmy coffee. He decided he wanted tea instead. Meg volunteered a turn at the stove.

"So how are your kids taking the romance?" I asked him.

"That's a lousy thing to ask," he complained. "And you did it in a lousy tone." He inspected Meg's back, at least from the waist down. "The girls understand that Federica's trying to turn them against me. But they know their father couldn't endure living a lie."

"That's a lot of understanding for four- and five-year-olds."

"You've got a hell of a sanctimonious tone for someone who eats Chinese takeout."

"Truce," I said.

"Okay." He leaned forward. "Is she some kind of gymnast? I've never seen feet move so fast. She must be causing a commotion out on the street." He thought some more. "Do you think she'll bring back a cop?"

"I'm sure she won't."

"If she does, I can't bail you out," Timmy said. "Federica's cut me off at the bank, too. I'm not even sure I would make a great character witness."

"That's okay." There would have been a car waiting on the street, probably with a driver. If I asked around the neighborhood, somebody might describe them.

"Would you like to have dinner with us?" Meg asked. "If you're not too angry."

"Sure. But let's go somewhere out of the neighborhood."

"Martick's?"

Timmy shrugged. Not wanting company.

"Fine," I said. "But I've got to make a call first." Neither of them took the hint to clear out. I used the wall phone and got the number of Greg Lord's hotel. He wasn't registered.

Charlie Kimball might know how to reach him. I rang the place in Connecticut and persuaded the maid to go collect him from outdoors. He came on sounding breathless.

"It's time I talked with your friend Greg," I said. "Can you contact him?"

He had me wait a moment and came back with a number in Washington. "He may be on the road. If it's urgent, use my name. They may track him down. Listen, you haven't told me what happened in New Hampshire."

"Last night wasn't a good time. This isn't either. It didn't go well."

"How sinister do you think Raab is?" Charlie asked, thinking he was changing the subject.

It was an odd word—sinister. A lot closer to the mark than "dishonest." How sinister? He sounded agitated, as if his rock wall had tumbled.

"The reason I ask," Charlie said, "is that my daughters weren't happy when I put the kibosh on their vacation scheme last night. Betsy left a note with the gardener. She and her sister caught a plane this afternoon at JFK. They've signed on to work for Raab for a week in Paris."

17

I HEARD CHARLIE KIMBALL SAY, "DO YOU THINK I SHOULD be concerned?" His tone was more tentative than I was used to.

"Have you spoken to Raab?" I asked.

"His secretary says he's out until this evening. I don't know . . ." His voice dwindled.

Conscious of Timmy's ears, I told Charlie: "See if you can reach Lucius Astenberg. He seems to have known Raab for a long time."

He said he would check and phone me back.

"You're mixing with your betters," Timmy Upham said. "Did you say Lucius Astenberg?"

"I've got to take a rain check on dinner," I said.

Timmy nodded as though he knew I had dumped him for one of my betters. He seemed content to sag at the counter, sipping his tea. Meg urged him up. "Come on, Timothy. Let's give Don his key back."

"Yeah. We've got to boogie. See you, Donald. Sorry about barging in." He gave me a toothy grin, as if his unfaithfulness paled beside my kinky sports.

"I'll see you at the shop tomorrow," I said. I got them onto the elevator and watched from the front windows as they crossed the street and headed toward West Broadway.

I tried Raab's office and got the tarty assistant, who said he would return at eight o'clock but might not want to conduct business this evening.

It was close to six-thirty. I couldn't raise Greg Lord

or anybody else at the number in Washington. I washed the cups and saucers thinking it hadn't taken much cunning to outmaneuver me.

At six-forty-five Charlie Kimball reported: "I told Lucius that I was trying to find a superior money manager for a friend. What did he think of Gustav Raab? Lucius absolutely vouched for Raab's integrity and ability. Perhaps my concern is misplaced."

He was asking a question, and I told him his concern wasn't misplaced. Just enough about New Hampshire without the crimson details. His voice sank to a whisper. "I had no idea. If I hadn't been willing to let Greg use you, my daughters wouldn't be involved."

"People don't get kidnapped onto flights at JFK," I said. "That means they went willingly. Read me Betsy's note."

He came back in a moment. "She said 'You've been bamboozled by your clever daughters, all in the family tradition. We're off to Paris to meet a Prince.' She put some details at the bottom. 'TWA Flight 804, JFK, arrives Paris six-fifty A.M. local time. Will call.' If I'd gotten this two hours ago, I could have had Raab arrested at the boarding gate."

He didn't say how but I believed him.

"Raab didn't go with," I said. "His office said he'll be back this evening."

"It's time Greg rolled the bastard up."

"It's time Greg steered clear of him." I told Charlie what I intended to do. He promised to track down Greg Lord.

It took a while using the flight number to check the schedule and make sure of the airport they were flying into. When I had that information, I woke up Bill Hinsdale in Paris. He reacted badly. "For God's sake, one o'clock in the morning! If you want an update on EC of Belgium, call back in ten hours at the office."

"I want you to meet a plane," I said.

He didn't hang up. "What?"

I gave him the flight's arrival time and other details. "They won't be expecting you. If it's a big plane, you might have trouble spotting them. You might want to make up a sign with their names."

He sighed. "It's nice your girlfriends are coming over, but couldn't they just go to a hotel?"

"You might want to take a friend with you. There may be somebody with them who won't like your interference."

"What are they smuggling?"

"Nothing. There's nothing illegal. Take them to your place and phone me."

"What if they don't want to come to my place?"

"Then have them phone their father from the airport."

"Okay, okay. Just tell me again that nobody's smuggling anything."

Gustav Raab sounded cheery. "Is something the matter, my dear boy? Elise said you were quite adamant. So I call you with my evening coat still on." He had taken time to put some music on. The *Kreutzer* Sonata was playing in the background. He must have needed a few minutes. After a date with Jerry, I wasn't supposed to leave phone messages.

"My friend Charlie Kimball is upset," I said. "He thinks you overruled him and hired his daughters for Paris. I assured him you were still right here in town."

"Why, I think I am!" He chortled, delighted with himself. "But the Misses Kimball are not? I do not understand. I assure you it is not my doing. But of course—of course I can understand why Mr. Kimball is upset."

"He was on the verge of calling the French consulate," I said. "I discouraged that."

"Yes, why create a disturbance? You imply that their plane is en route now? That may be a stroke of

123

good fortune. Bruno went over this morning to arrange meetings. I'm certain that tomorrow he can find your friends' hotel and make certain all is well. Have you decided whether you can join me?"

I didn't answer, and he prodded. "The clients would be delighted with your perspective. I think it could benefit both of us."

"I'll join you," I said. With the girls in Mullins's care, I would go to the moon if he told me to.

There was a chance I could stay home. If Bill Hinsdale came through. I was asleep on the couch, drink in hand, when the phone rang at five A.M. He should have called by two. His angry voice explained that he couldn't call then, because the big blond guy had brought along a man from the CRS. That was the security police. There had been a misunderstanding at the airport over Monsieur Hinsdale's residency papers, an embarrassing mix-up that required the officer from the CRS to detain Monsieur Hinsdale for a couple of hours. The big blond guy met the girls as they got off the plane. "I'm still at DeGaulle," Bill said. "Marie had to bring our papers out here. That bastard has important friends."

18

It was forty-eight hours before Raab and I got to Paris, where it was cool and drizzly. Bruno Mullins met the plane, and we took a cab through dreary green streets. "How is the Mayol?" Raab wanted to know.

Mullins replied, "Standards have slipped." He ignored me, leaning over the seat back and handing Raab a yellow pad. "Here is the appointment list. Kostelanetz is this evening. You see de Bora tomorrow. Prince Ricard has not said so, but I believe that he wants us to acquire a group of publications in Rome."

"That would be the same magazines from last year?"

"No, another buyer was found for those. This would be a smaller concern with fashion and computer magazines. The seller wants twelve times cash flow."

Raab grunted. "What do you think of that, Donald?"

"It sounds expensive."

Bruno Mullins's blue eyes met mine. "It is *low* for the industry, Herr McCarry. Spiegelsgrupen AG paid more in January for a less dynamic group."

Did I give a damn how much Raab paid for magazines? I gave a damn about not letting Mullins get the last word. I said, "It takes a long time to recoup your money at those prices."

Mullins shrugged with his forehead and turned

125

back to watch the road. Raab patted my raincoat, which was folded across my knee. "We are long-term investors, my dear friend. We can afford to wait for an acquisition to deliver a profit. Still—the price is a bit steep, yes, Bruno? We can be long-term investors without paying too much for the privilege." He chuckled.

Mullins didn't. He said, "Ricard believes that this property could be resold within a year for thirty percent more than our cost."

"We will hear his proposal, Bruno."

Mullins accepted a moral victory by sneering at me in the mirror.

"Tell me, Bruno, what are the girls doing? Donald is eager to be reunited with them."

"What are they doing? Spending money. Whose? I don't know, perhaps their father's. Certainly more than they are earning in your employ, Herr Raab."

Raab sat back, beaming. "You see Donald, no need for concern."

For two days Raab and I had shared an agreeable fiction that Mullins had misunderstood his boss's exchange with Charlie Kimball. So he had pulled strings to get clearances and messengered airline tickets and a cash advance in Raab's name to Stacy at the gallery. Bill Hinsdale had been the fault of some lunatic at the CRS; Mullins professed ignorance about the episode. We were all great friends. Raab had chatted at me all the way across the Atlantic. On arrival, Mullins hadn't tried to break my arm.

They were adaptable. Having the girls close had been meant to keep Charlie Kimball in line. No need for a leash on Donald after Jerry had her fun. But they adjusted deftly to my unexpected health.

The rain picked up as we crossed a bridge and crept along the quai du Louvre. We swung a couple of blocks up from the river. The hotel was a Gothic castle at one end of a big square. Under the front portico we unloaded suitcases while water cascaded from the battlements in sooty torrents. I said to Raab, "I thought they tore down the Bastille."

"My dear boy, the Mayol has five stars! Bruno and I always stay here. The manager is a dear friend."

A skinny old man dressed like a minor general in Napoleon's army showed us to the lift without stopping at the reception desk. He and Raab jabbered happily in French. I picked up fragments as the old man, whose name was Henri, cursed the Socialists and sang the praises of the Transportation Union, which had been on strike at the behest of the Communists.

The lift was an iron cage that ascended from the lobby to a mezzanine within an open framework. I managed to look down at the expanse of paisley carpet in time to see Greg Lord enter the lobby.

He had sat four rows behind us on the flight, but I'd worried that we had lost him in traffic.

The cage rattled on up to the fifth floor, and the old man banged the door open. Mullins strode down the gilt-trimmed hall, letting Henri drag the suitcases.

"Our usual suites?" Raab inquired.

"Yours, *ja*," Mullins said. "The girls are between us. The stockbroker has the small room."

Henri got doors unlocked and lights flicked on, cursing softly. My room was fourth from the end of the corridor. The gray afternoon made the corners dim, even with the candelabra casting a sallow glow. Raab rolled in, paid Henri off, and shooed him away. "Come the revolution, my friend! . . . Henri believes that one day his comrades will rule. When they do, of course, Henri will still carry other people's bags. He does not know this."

I pulled the lace curtains apart but the room didn't get much brighter. Raab pointed beyond the double doors and faux balcony. An imposing building occupied the opposite side of the square. *"L'Opéra.* Behind are shops where your friends may have spent their pay."

"Did Mullins chaperone them?"

"I doubt that. Bruno has a limited interest in women." So that I didn't misunderstand, he said, "An intense interest, but one-dimensional."

"I see."

"Would you like to have a nap and then join me downstairs for an early dinner? We must prepare for tonight's client."

We had done little on the flight from New York but discuss Raab's clients. He spoke in a shorthand of nicknames that became a blur of meaningless "Das" and "Popos" and "Mishas" in my head. Their financial interests Raab described in general terms while giving no useful details—and nothing that helped me get a feel for the clients behind the portfolios. When he wasn't spinning a nonsensical filigree of transactions, we talked stocks. Latin banks and Asian airlines had caught his fancy, and I tried to camouflage my ignorance of both groups by mumbling about exchange rates.

I wondered how long he was going to keep up the charade of the happy client and his stockbroker.

"I would like to see Stacy and Betsy," I said.

"Of course!"

We went into the hall, and he gestured to the door between Mullins's room and his own.

I knocked.

Nobody answered, and I rapped with more force.

Raab shrugged. "They are out. Perhaps Bruno gave them the afternoon off. I will ask after my nap."

I went back to the gray room and unfolded my suit bag but took nothing out. Mullins would keep the girls tucked away until he knew how much he and Raab had to fear from Charlie. If their friends nosed around New York and Connecticut, not everything they learned about Charles Kimball and Tracer Minerals would add up. Charlie had secrets, if he could get on the phone at night and reach a Treasury agent.

But then . . . when Greg Lord's people dug into Raab Capital and Rain Tree Capital, the pieces they found wouldn't fit seamlessly. Bill Hinsdale hadn't been able to come up with much on Raab. The family background pointed to a man born to his profession, but it had the gossamer texture of official biography. If Bill had sampled ten contacts in France, every one who recognized the name might have known basically the same quaint story.

And would I ever find a Swiss banker who acknowledged training Mullins?

Well, maybe. Mullins would be a natural at keeping secrets. If Geneva or Zurich had a blabbermouth, Mullins would pull his tongue out.

I lay down on the bed to think and woke up in near darkness.

The room caught a dingy glow from the square, which made the furniture look shabby and the room unclean. Somebody loomed over the bed. Hair brushed my face, and the bedside light came on.

"I waited till you woke up," Stacy said. Without catching a breath, she rushed on. "I've missed you so much, Donald. Three days is a long time."

I sat up groggily. "Are you all right?"

"Of *course!* We've been having the time of our lives. But I've missed you every minute. Sometimes the dresses and shoes are so gorgeous I forget to miss you, but just for an instant."

She looked great, hair drifting over one shoulder, smelling of perfume and August rain. She had on a blue-striped shirtdress that I had seen before and gold snowflake earrings that I didn't remember.

I told her how good it was to see her, not exaggerating too much. She pushed me down and applied a complicated kiss. "At least we agree on that," she said finally. "I'm sorry I ducked out on you. But I had a feeling you and Daddy both were going to be a pain in the ass about this trip."

"Have you talked to your father?"

"A couple of times. He's not very talkative." She frowned. "He doesn't usually stay angry at me for more than a day."

He'd been beside himself when I left. He couldn't tell his daughters what he wanted to, and small talk must have been torture.

"Yesterday," she said, "he told me to trust you implicitly and do whatever you said." She smiled skeptically, as if he couldn't possibly have meant it. "Have you gotten him to sign over the family fortune yet?"

His trust stirred an unexpected emotion in me, a flush of gratitude. And a whisper of unease, as if someone had just tied a leash around my neck. I asked, "Did Charlie say you should tell me that?"

"He said to tell you he had the utmost confidence in you. How did you guess?"

Because I knew Charlie was a crafty devil.

"Where is Betsy?"

"In the room, showering."

I settled against the headboard. "How did you get in here?"

"The door wasn't locked."

I glanced at the nightstand. The key was where Henri had left it. I remembered checking that the door had latched after Raab left.

She leaned on an elbow and played with my hair. "As much as I'm enjoying myself, this is a half-assed way Raab runs his business," she said. "We haven't done a lick of work and nobody seems to mind. That may change now that chubs himself has arrived. Do you think?"

"It may," I agreed. I tried to sound casual. "Has Bruno been keeping an eye on you?"

"Not at all. He doesn't care if we work, play, or drink ourselves blind."

Not good news. Somebody would be watching. If not Mullins, we had to spot someone else before I got very far in planning our escape. A lot depended on whether Mullins could call on the security police again.

"My business with Raab may not work out," I said. "In which case we might want to leave in a hurry. Keep it in mind."

"It sounds like you expect trouble."

"It's possible. Another thing, if you see Greg Lord hanging around, pretend you don't know him. Tell Betsy."

"What's he doing here?"

"A case of some kind, I guess."

"Involving you—or Raab?—or—?"

"Maybe he's on vacation. I don't know. Just ignore him."

"You aren't telling me everything."

"I didn't ask you to come over here," I said. "Neither did Charlie."

"If you're worried, why don't we just leave now?"

I didn't know how she would take hearing that Mullins wouldn't let us. Not all three of us. For as long as possible I wanted to keep up the illusion of cordiality. Three informal hostages beat having one or two tucked away where I couldn't find them. "So far, the business with Raab is going well," I said. "Why lose the account if I don't have to? For that matter, why should you drop your shopping binge?"

"I think I understand. You're worried that Mr. Raab will catch on to the fact you've been bullshitting him."

"What?"

"Your great expertise on international investing must be wearing thin, huh, Donald?" There was more than a little contempt in her tone.

"That's part of it," I conceded.

"I should have caught on to you by now. You never take a straight road if there's a crooked one." She got off the bed and left. The door closed softly. She wasn't angry, just disappointed again.

Five minutes later Raab called. "Would you join me in the Verdum Restaurant in twenty minutes? We will go from there to meet our client."

I showered and shaved in ten minutes. That left time to play. My Econo Guide to France was in a side pocket of the suit bag. I turned on the lamp on the room's tiny desk and found a map page. It showed roads and rail lines, with points of interest number coded. Versailles rated a 2, while Napoleon's tomb was 16. The Paris map was on too large a scale for my purposes, so I thumbed to a layout of the northwest quadrant of the country. Paris was a bull's-eye near the lower right corner. A major rail line stretched north from the city, branching many times. If you wanted to leave Paris and make a beeline for the coast, it looked like either Boulogne or Calais was a jumping-off point for channel ferries to England. The text on the next page showed that trains left pretty much hourly from the Gare du Nord, which could be reached by the Metro system.

After some thought, I got a pen and circled the Boulogne dot discreetly, then turned to the city map and did the same with the Gare du Nord. Then I closed the guide and left it on the desk with the pen holding the place.

Raab's pet bullethead didn't come to dinner. The hotel's Verdum Restaurant, which had ornate sconces on the walls between columns of red brocade, mirrors on the ceiling, and a fountain with a half-dozen fauns exposing themselves at midcourt, was almost deserted. It was five-thirty, too late for lunch and too early for civilized dining. Greg Lord sat two tables away, as subtle as a police whistle.

19

DMITRI KOSTELANETZ RESEMBLED A MIDDLE-SIZED WHITE bear drawn back to its full imposing height of five foot eight. Not tall for a skinny man but substantial for a bear. The forehead was low and deeply lined, topped by a ruff of snowy hair that was cut by a few black tracks. There was no demarcation between the forehead and the nose, which flattened into a lumpy pink snout. The mouth was wide and heavy-lipped. The lightly curled fingers and the backs of the hands were matted with white hair. His massive chest seemed designed to display medals or campaign ribbons but wore only a yellowed shirt and a black jacket with frayed lapels.

He welcomed us into his mansion's foyer with brusque formality. "Monsieur Raab, Monsieur McCarry. You are ten minutes late." The accent was thickly Slavic, with a glaze of French slurring the r's. Mullins rated only a glance.

"Our car was not ready when it should have been," Raab said, causing Mullins to stare at nothing. He had arrived at our table at seven-thirty, but Raab had drunk a second brandy before we set out in the rented Audi. The drive to the city's western suburbs had taken twenty minutes.

Neither Raab nor Mullins had said much to prepare me for Kostelanetz. He was retired, an offspring of a banking family that had lost its wealth between 1914 and 1949 as control of the homeland shifted several times. "Each successive ruler confiscated what the others had missed," Raab had confided at dinner. "The public treasury always needed infusions of plunder."

Greg Lord wasn't close enough to pick that up. I wondered what he was making of Gustav Raab. The Treasury's toughest agent had been offhand with Charlie Kimball and me the previous morning in New York. "Tax evasion is a competitive business. Every entrepreneur in this industry is angling for a new way to beat the rules." Too offhand, I thought. But Charlie acted reassured. I still hadn't told him about Petrus or Parker. Greg Lord didn't seem to think it was the ideal moment either.

Kostelanetz's mansion was part of a group of huge sandstone houses standing right against a narrow sidewalk across from a heavily wooded park. The fronts looked both substantial and opaque. You weren't supposed to guess who lived here.

The foyer was big enough to have made a comfortable parlor, tiled in large alternating diamonds of black and white slate. It had its own fireplace, which gave off a smell of wet ashes, a sofa and two chairs that had seen happier days. On the walls were a few paintings in the style of David that showed Napoleon dressed in a flowing Roman gown receiving the admiration of court functionaries or, farther down the room, the Muses.

Once he got over being miffed at our lateness, Kostelanetz led us down the hall to a study. The walls were covered with oak paneling decorated with carvings of grapevines and pineapples. The floor was scuffed parquet covered with faded rugs. The furniture was large, solid, and long used. Kostelanetz moved in halting steps like a man in pain. He stopped at a library table stacked with books, bottles of liquor, and stemware. "What is your pleasure, Gustav?"

Raab asked for a brandy while Mullins and I abstained. My head was buzzing from dinner.

Kostelanetz handed Raab a snifter and poured generously. Throughout the activity his left arm hung at his side. The hand holding the bottle was steady.

Raab bubbled appreciatively but didn't get to drink right away. As he sat down, Kostelanetz demanded, "Show me what you've brought."

Raab went through a fussy routine of setting the glass precisely on the center of a round, leather-topped table. Mullins handed him an attaché case, which the boss balanced on plump knees. He snapped it open and extracted the top document. From where I stood the case appeared to be full of loose computer printouts and wire-bound file folders. Raab handed a wad of bar-striped paper to Kostelanetz, who read while standing.

As the silence grew, Raab fidgeted. Mullins stood with his hands at his sides, almost pinching the seams of his pants.

"The overall return appears to be satisfactory," Kostelanetz said.

Raab nodded enthusiastically. "Thank you, sir. We've delivered approximately two and one-half percentage points more than the Standard & Poor's five hundred for the last nine months. That is also almost two percentage points better than the return from a composite of seventeen world markets."

Kostelanetz glanced at the papers again. His breathing was audible from a dozen feet away. "Yes, I see. Success is to be commended, Gustav. But are we comfortable with the level of risk we incur? Capital that is lost is lost forever."

"The overall risk is quite modest, Mitya, because we are so widely diversified." Raab looked uncomfortable.

Kostelanetz's thick white brows rose in a shrug. "Small pieces, yes, yes." He looked at me suddenly. "Which would you rather own, Mr. McCarry? The Hope Diamond or fifty smaller stones of approximately the same total value?"

"It would depend on how I planned to use them—and whether I had a heavy-breathing buyer lined up for the big stone," I said, wondering—without the faintest clue—where the Hope Diamond reposed and how much it was worth. I tried to think as Kostelanetz might. "If I wanted to move them quietly, one stone would be easier but an all-or-nothing risk. If you had fifty stones and wanted to slip them by customs or the border police, you could move them in ten lots and not suffer a total loss if one or two were intercepted."

From the corner of my eye, I'd been watching Raab for a clue to my performance, but he was expressionless. I thought I'd done it just about right.

Kostelanetz gestured to Raab with his good arm. "Your young friend talks like a smuggler rather than a stockbroker. What is this nonsense about border police? Emergency crossings are part of Europe's past. We do not live in Latin America or Lebanon." He said the last more or less to me.

Raab held his knees together like a schoolgirl with a bladder problem.

I didn't like being flunked when the rules hadn't been announced. "Small stones also attract less attention at home," I said.

Kostelanetz shrugged. "Very well. But attention—the perception that what one possesses is unique—heightens a buyer's affection. Anyone may possess a fine stone, set in a fancy pendant, but the owner of a *unique* stone becomes himself unique."

Low marks again for McCarry. He had given me a

cue with the approving murmur about "small pieces" and then jumped with both boots on my answer.

Waving his good arm dismissively, Kostelanetz said, "Your answer is correct, however. Diversification is of benefit even to those of us who expect never again in this lifetime to steal across a frontier. Ha, steal across with our fortune in our bowels! A Hope Diamond may inspire passion among buyers, but tomorrow perhaps their passion will be just one-tenth less than today. Then what will happen to the price? A unique property cannot enjoy a wide market—only a handful of men or women can ever be bidders. When we want to sell, the price may not be there for us. Whereas small pieces can be let go over time."

He nodded as if he had disposed of the subject.

"It's easier to sell a hundred shares of stock than to sell the entire company," I said, nodding back. He couldn't imagine anybody putting him on. So I had to be an idiot. I nodded at Raab too.

Raab piped up. "No more than fifteen percent of our assets are in any country, Mitya. Indeed, the greatest concentration is our forty-two percent in Europe. That is exceedingly well dispersed—"

"And impractical to change, I agree."

"By next year the percentage will be smaller in any case," Raab said. "Growth rates in the United States and Asian portfolios are faster. Though Monsieur McCarry has helped us nicely on the European side. The second-best-performing stock in our portfolio in this quarter is his selection, Electronics Corporation of Belgium. It is up seventy percent in Belgian francs since June."

Kostelanetz gave me a look that said *blind luck* and returned to reading the printout. He asked a couple of questions about the outlook for industrial and mining companies, articulated his reactions in grunts as Raab explained short ideas at length. Every working day I heard people talking through their hats. On most days

I did it myself. So I had an ear for the stuff and estimated that about twenty-five percent of what Raab told Kostelanetz came out of a hat.

After fifteen minutes, Kostelanetz told Mullins and me to leave. I followed Mullins down the hall. He shuffled his feet in the foyer for a minute, then glanced at his watch. "This will take time," he said mostly to himself. "I will stretch my legs. You must join me, McCarry. We will talk."

He opened the door and I saw that he had in mind the park across the street. It looked and smelled like a very nice park to stroll in, but not with Bruno.

"I'm not up for exercise," I said. "Still feeling the time change."

The chairs didn't look inviting, but I settled into a wingback. It was a blockish, ugly thing with lion's-claw feet. The style was American, designed for a Revolutionary War hero named Cadwalader, but I had read that some of the pieces had been turning up in Europe at fancy auctions.

Mullins said, "Do you hope to remain associated with Herr Raab?"

"I do."

"It is possible," he said thoughtfully. "But I doubt that you will succeed."

He closed the door behind him, and his heels clicked down the sidewalk and across the road.

Kostelanetz and Raab took their time. After fifteen minutes I got up and stared at the adorations of Napoleon. That grew old in a hurry. The fireplace was more interesting. In gray stone carvings, fat cherubim on the wing frolicked on the sides, teasing wolves and nymphs. Centered above the opening was a solemn face of a woman with classical features, large downcast eyes, a full lower lip.

She had beauty and an air of tranquillity.

She had snakes for hair.

* * *

We got back to the hotel at nine-thirty. Raab had been less than his bubbly self. Taciturn, lips rigid in a petulant bow. He headed directly up to his room. Mullins disappeared into a small corridor of shops. The bar behind the lobby was just getting up to speed. I got a tiny table and ordered coffee and sambuca. Stacy and Betsy sat at the bar, entertained by three young admirers. For a moment I let myself feel dumped, abandoned, brushed off, then looked around without seeing Greg Lord and felt better.

If I could separate the girls from their friends, right now would be a good time to run off for the airport. Let Mullins chase the trains to Boulogne and Calais. I wondered if we would get more than a mile down the road.

A fat middle-aged woman sat at the piano and began drumming chords and warbling *"Non, je ne regrette rien"* without interrupting the room's clatter of high voices. For a while she made a bid for control with *"Monsieur Saint Pierre,"* and the balance tee-tered. But the crowd was younger than she. When a half-dozen hooting tourists from Akron rolled in, she gave up and settled for turning out background music.

I tried to catch Stacy's eye.

She hadn't looked my way since I'd come in. The boys were too young for her. So we were in the punish-Don mode. Betsy was sitting with her back mostly to me. She wore a silky black dress that was too old for her but had one of the boys slack-jawed.

I took my sambuca over and wedged a shoulder between a dark-haired young man in a linen jacket and Stacy. "Good evening," I said.

Her nose twitched. She could pretend I was a stranger. She didn't. Perhaps she remembered something I had said about getting out of town. "Everyone comes to Paris," she said with a worldly sigh.

Betsy patted me on the shoulder. "Hello, brother-in-law. Stacy says you hate Paris. You should have come with us to Disco Pyramid. Habibi and Cha-Cha showed us the sights. Habibi works for Radio Monte Carlo, and Cha-Cha exports wine. Or his father does."

Two of the three boys grinned at me but didn't sort themselves out.

"I wouldn't want to separate you from your friends. But it's time to travel." I said the last softly to Stacy.

"This is Don McCarry, a tiresome fellow," she explained to anyone who cared.

"McCarry?" The male voice was almost in my left ear. It belonged to the boy I had nudged aside. He sounded pleased. "McCarry! I thought you looked familiar."

The eyes were close-set and dark, the forehead about as high as a hatband. The lips were full and sensuous. Great material for modeling men's bathing suits. He said, "I didn't think we would meet up again so soon. You didn't tell me you get over here."

It had been several weeks since he dropped into my office, a kid in a bomber jacket with a two million–dollar check.

Imrie de Wohl slapped the shoulder of one of the darker boys. "Hey, Cha-Cha, this dude is my stock-broker. How have we done, Mr. McCarry? I haven't gotten home to check the mail."

"You're doing fine," I said, not knowing. It takes a big shock to knock a list of stocks out of my head. But Imrie de Wohl had done it.

"It's some coincidence!" he said. "I hope you're not sore we were trying to pick up your ladies."

"It's a tribute to your good taste."

"So—do we have to go?" Stacy asked.

"You know how the Riklises are—great parties but they demand punctuality," I said. "We wouldn't want Mrs. Riklis to throw a fit."

"I should hope not," Stacy said dryly.

"She makes such a spectacle," Betsy agreed. Stacy hadn't asked who the Riklises were, so Betsy didn't.

She had most of Cha-Cha's attention, though he glanced furtively at Imrie.

"Hey, so you guys are going to a party," Imrie said. "You didn't mention that. 'Bibi could drive you. He could drive all of us. Where's your party located?"

I remembered a name from the guidebook. "The Marais."

"We could *walk* there! Right, Cha-Cha?"

The other boy's features contorted. "Why should we? They got nothing but Jews and fag bars."

"He's right," Habibi said.

"Never mind that," Imrie objected. "My stockbroker and his ladies have a party there. It's only courtesy that we take them. This man—he's gonna make me a lot of money."

The other two shook their heads.

I was wondering how I was going to get out of this when Stacy pointed to her red challis skirt. "You don't expect me to go to an elegant Riklis party wearing this?"

I registered dismay. "How long will it take you to change?"

"Ten minutes. Twenty if I shower."

"Maybe I'll take a shower, too," Betsy said with a quirky smile.

"Me too," said Cha-Cha.

Betsy pushed him back. "You haven't been that charming."

"Okay," I said, "we'll take a half hour. Imrie, you don't want to wait. I'll have the concierge call a taxi."

"It's okay—really."

"I won't hear of it. Let's have breakfast here tomorrow and go over your portfolio. You'll be happy."

He looked like he couldn't have cared less. We were at the point where he couldn't insist any further without sounding pushy. I couldn't refuse any further without seeming ungrateful.

We polished off our drinks and said good night. The

lobby was bustling with couples heading out for a night on the town. Betsy grabbed my arm and started to say something. "Save your questions," I said as we waited for the elevator. As we ascended, the iron cage gave me a good view of the lobby. Imrie and his friends didn't appear.

There was no light under Mullins's door but a bright sliver under Raab's. Muffled voices spoke in German. I followed the girls into their room and closed the door. A sitting area held a faded love seat, two chairs, and a petite breakfast table. In the bedroom, the *Opéra's* lights glowed from across the square.

"This is more than a business problem with Raab," Stacy said.

"Yes."

"Spill it."

"Robert Petrus was murdered up in Merrimack. So was the fellow he was investigating."

She stared without comprehension. Betsy said, "That smart-alecky little guy got killed?"

"What does that have to do with Raab?" Stacy said.

"Mullins was involved in killing Petrus, probably in both murders."

Stacy asked coolly, "And Raab?"

"He gives Mullins orders," I said.

"But to kill people?" Stacy said.

"There's more to it, but I don't know what." Nazi treasure wouldn't lead to the Paris suburbs. The Romanovs' fortune was on display in the Kremlin. Yet Lord had been just as happy we were coming to Paris. This was where he expected to learn something.

"Raab is not a friend," I said. "Whatever Greg Lord wants to find out, Raab wants kept secret."

Betsy's face was pale. The holiday had turned ugly. "Are we going home?"

"Do you have your passports?" I went to the balcony window and pointed to the colonnaded building on the side of the square. We wouldn't get far making a run for it tonight. But tomorrow morning, when we were all going about our business, there might be a chance. "See the doorway nearest the street? I'm going to round up a car. When I drive by at ten-thirty tomorrow morning, you two be ready to hop in. You'll have to leave your luggage. Just slip away from whatever's going on."

"Haven't you got a meeting tomorrow morning?" Stacy said. "Mullins was making appointments yesterday."

I had forgotten. I didn't even know when or where the next client was to be entertained. "Do you know the details?" I asked.

She shook her head.

"Maybe Raab will tell us." From the hall, I closed their door silently, skulked down and unlocked the door to my own room. I switched on the light, threw my jacket and necktie on the bed. Back in the hall, looking ready to call it a night, I tapped on Raab's door.

He was wearing a maroon paisley dressing gown that made him look like the comics page's Little King, all belly and goatee. The round face's usual good humor was missing. He looked unhappy and uneasy.

"Sorry to disturb you," I said. "I wondered about our schedule for tomorrow morning. There's a young client of mine down in the bar—amazing who you meet in Paris. I promised him a few minutes to go over his holdings."

His smile was an indifferent flicker. "Of course. We have a meeting at the hotel at nine-thirty with Prince Ricard. It should not reach beyond eleven-thirty. Perhaps your client would enjoy lunch at Taillevent. It is in the Eighth Arrondissement and is my favorite."

"You won't need me later?"

"Not until mid-afternoon. An hour's preparation would be in order for our five o'clock meeting. Put your thinking cap on, Donald, and offer me your best American stock."

When I thanked him, he nodded and closed the door. He seemed detached, almost demoralized. I wondered if he had caught hell from Kostelanetz.

I went next door, talked in whispers. "We'll make it one-thirty. Now I'm going downstairs."

"Why can't we just call the police?" Betsy said. "They can't keep us here when we don't want to stay."

"A friend of mine tried to intercept you at the airport. He was arrested."

"Why don't we go to the embassy?"

"That's an option for tomorrow. But to get there we've got to get more than a block from the hotel, which I don't think we would tonight. If the police didn't have a man pick us up, your boyfriends would."

Stacy took charge. "If we've got only one chance, we should make it pay. Let's get some sleep, Bets." She looked at me pointedly. "It isn't Donald's fault that we're here. We should have been more wary of geeks bearing plane tickets. But Bruno was *so cute* with that brush cut and stern demeanor."

Betsy smiled. "And cement teeth, for biting heads off rodents."

"You like him, too? But he can't love both of us." She sat on the bed and wrapped an arm around her sister. The pale-green eyes watched me as I left.

There was a message in her look. She would be more disappointed in me than usual if I ducked out on them.

144

20

OLD JACKIE McCARRY WOULD HAVE DONE IT IN A minute. He'd always said that sticky situations weren't for sticking around in. Sticky situations could be defined broadly, to include the wife, offspring, steady work, or other demand on his emotions.

So Don McCarry wasn't his father's son, I thought, not really believing it.

I collected my suit jacket and went downstairs. Only Imrie was still in the bar. I went over and stood beside him. "Damnedest funny thing," I said. "We got upstairs and found out the party's tomorrow night. Betsy decided she's beat, so they're turning in. I checked with the client I'm over here with. We've got business at nine-thirty. How do you feel about breakfast at eight?"

"Bloody unfriendly." He ran a hand through oily black hair. "That's not to say I don't care what you've been doing with my lolly. Have you got something on for the rest of the day?"

"I'm pledged for a couple of hours at the modern museum, whatever it's called."

"The Beaubourg? It's got all the plumbing on the outside, a sight, really."

"I should be finished by three if we could get together for a drink."

"Why not? I'm over at the Ritz."

"It's a date. Do you know a good night spot near here?"

"This isn't hot enough for you?" The middle-aged warbler had finished her stand and slumped at a table near the piano, eating dinner. Imrie sipped his drink. "I see your point, mate. If it's girls you want, try Quasimodo, over on Île de la Cité."

"How far is that?"

"Ten-minute cab ride. Be careful. Not all the girls are nature's product." He lighted a cigarette, waved it. "I would escort you, but I promised to wait here for Cha-Cha and 'Bibi. Since we couldn't get invited to your party, they're phoning around for one that will take us."

I nodded as if I believed him. "I'm sure you'll find something."

"I hope so. An evening without a party is *so* barren."

I said good night and headed for the street. The doorman waved a cab up, and I used the business of getting inside to look around for Cha-Cha but couldn't spot him. Habibi was sitting in a pale Renault across the street. He hung with us as a single erratic headlight on the quayside expressway and across a bridge. The side streets looked good at minding their own business, with stone balconies too narrow for busybodies to stand on and windows solidly shuttered. The driver almost stopped to squeeze into an alley. Halfway down, he jerked to a sudden halt. Three girls with moussed hair burst from a hidden door, propelled by a blast of music. Above the door glowed a green neon hump. There was no name. I climbed out and paid off the driver.

It looked as though I had boxed myself in. The alley ended twenty yards ahead at a vine-covered wall. The only opening in the wall was a tall archway blocked by an iron gate. The girls who had blown out of the club spilled toward the top of the alley, walking on either side of my taxi, which lurched backward and almost smashed into Habibi speeding around the corner.

The door opened again. Two men in shiny suits hurried out and turned toward the alley's dead end. They acted as though they had a destination. If I ditched Habibi, it should look accidental. While he and the taxi backed and squeezed, I tagged after the two men. One of them pulled back a cuff and checked his wrist twice within a brisk dash. His companion made a dismissing gesture but hurried as well.

They reached the gate, which opened at the first man's touch. I went through on their heels, ignored except for an imperious glance. There was a wide, enclosed garden and through a curtain of trees shone the lights of a building. As they dashed off through the garden, I hung back. Habibi had driven halfway down the alley and had gotten out. He peered in the door at Quasimodo, ignoring a short-haired girl in a red skirt and tank top who gestured for him to move the car.

He asked questions I couldn't hear, and she shook her head. He looked around desperately.

So did I. The two men had gone down a hedged path to broad steps that led to an ornate entrance of some sort. On either side of me, other paths curved away through tall plantings between which dimly lighted pieces of statuary stared down with the vague arrogance of centuries. If I went straight, Habibi might reach the gate in time to see me. I bolted down the winding gallery on the left.

When the gate clanged, I had gone to ground in a thicket of laurel behind a pillar bearing a classical bust. From where I squatted I could watch a fair stretch of the path, almost back to the iron gate.

Steps sounded, and Habibi came along the flagstones. He had a good bloodhound's nose. Not only did he choose the right path. He slowed as he approached the Roman bust as if smelling sweat.

He stopped and stared intently.

Went on. Fifty feet down the gallery, he paused again. Pivoted feverishly. Took a step toward a life-size figure that looked like Diana. Stopped and listened. He was a portrait in frustration. The shrug was worthy of a silent-screen star. Hands in his pockets, he shuffled on, the hunt abandoned, giving himself up to the stroll. Not altogether convincing.

I stayed put. After a few minutes, the gate clanged. Nobody else came along. I settled onto my knees.

Five minutes later he came around from the opposite direction, looking worried without having to pretend. He'd had enough time to scout the adjacent building. He must have begun to suspect that the quarry had gotten lost inside.

Or had slipped into Quasimodo without the girl noticing.

But his instincts told him I was close by. If he paid heed and began quartering the garden, his chance of flushing me was excellent.

If the instinct spoke when he passed within five feet of me, he ignored it. Eyes intent on the flagstones, mind perhaps working on an excuse for Imrie, he disappeared toward the wall. The gate clanged again.

I waited, but he didn't return.

He might be staked out near Quasimodo. Or near the gate. Or driving easy circles through a district he had to know better than I did.

I left cover. The stone stairway opened onto a bright arcade of elegant shops, their windows packed with marzipan, women's gowns, jewelry, and wristwatches. Despite the hour, they were still going strong for customers wearing Arab getups. At the end of the arcade was a vast marble-and-gilt lobby with lines at the check-in desks. It looked as if the Kuwaiti Chamber of Commerce had just blown into town.

I got a taxi in front of the hotel and crossed the Seine to Bill Hinsdale's neighborhood.

Marie was having none of my old-college-buddies routine. "You could have gotten Bill hurt, and I don't like it," she said, splashing coffee in front of me. She was a tall, dark-haired woman he had picked up somewhere on the road one year. She had broad farmer's hands, long legs, solid hips, massive breasts, and strong opinions. A couple of boys not long out of diapers romped in the kitchen, mixing it up with a kitten.

"I'm sorry, Marie. I didn't think there was any danger."

"I don't believe you. You knew that Swiss robot would be there."

"He may not be Swiss," I murmured.

"Oh, but he is." She divided her attention between me and the kitchen. "Bill heard his French." She paused. "Bill should not have been arrested."

"I was detained, not arrested," Bill said cheerfully. He sat at the dining room table, wearing sweatpants and a turtleneck, hair spiky from the shower. "It's okay, Marie. This will teach me not to answer the telephone after midnight. How are you doing, chum?" He stretched a big hand across the table. "Hey, sweetheart, what do you say to a Lillet? Three glasses?"

She brought a chilled bottle of amber wine and martini glasses.

"Here's to prosperity," he said, and we sipped. "What about those girls?"

"They're at the Mayol, shopping and partying."

"You wanted me to rescue them from that?" He laughed. "That guy Mullins is a beaut. I hadn't got within two feet of the gate, waving my 'Stacy & Betsy' poster, when Mullins and this little monkey from the regional security police step out of the crowd and the cops hustle me off. They were ready for interference. But you say everything's okay?"

"Not exactly."

He had trouble meaning it when he frowned. He was a cheerful fixer of problems, a scientific workman, rather than a worrier about them. "Are you in trouble?"

"It could be a little sticky."

"And you still say you haven't smuggled anything?"

Marie rolled her eyes and went to rescue the cat.

"Is your problem tied to Gustav Raab?" Bill asked. "I couldn't dig up anything more that sounded useful. He strikes me as the kind of guy who could be a king-size fraud."

"He seems to have clients who are real. I've met a couple. Does the name Dmitri Kostelanetz mean anything to you? I think he's Eastern European."

Bill shook his head.

"What about de Bora, as in Prince Ricard? Or Imrie de Wohl?" I added a couple of surnames I thought I had extracted from Raab's babbling on the flight over.

"There's a de Bora family in Tuscany. Old handgun manufacturers. Pretty famous. They supply a lot of NATO sidearms. Do you think that's your de Bora?"

"I don't know. We're meeting tomorrow morning." Since I didn't know anything about de Bora except his interest in a magazine group, I described Kostelanetz and his house.

Bill merely shrugged. "I'll ask around if you want. Europe is a tangled place. You don't always know who you're doing business with. Even less often who's got money and who hasn't. The marchesa may be on her uppers, or she may own a modern little computer-assembly plant."

Marie came back and sat down. "You must blame the decline of the aristocracy for our chaos. When the Continent lost its common link of the nobility, it lost its cohesion. So today people look for identity in political doctrines or in fanatic cults and secret societies."

She was adamant as usual, interjecting her concern of the day into any conversation she came across. "So—you see, even war is more dreadful. You did not have total war when chivalry remained the code. Courtesies were observed in combat. Chivalry was the code of the aristocracy."

I wasn't sure I followed the connections from one point to another.

Bill chuckled. "Marie is worried about the Masons taking over."

"Does that come under the heading of secret society or fanatic cult?"

She didn't appreciate ridicule. "Ask the Italians. P two were running a government within the government in Rome—as Opus Dei does still in Spain."

"Was the aristocracy preferable?" I said.

"You knew who they were, and it was not a one-way street, privilege without obligation. Today"—she shrugged—"aristocracy is money, nothing more. Apart from spendthrift children and fools, the people with money are seldom visible. That makes them hard to control. There is no social quid pro quo. The old aristocracy in Europe had obligations tied to their privileges. Yes, they were exempt from taxation in France, but in time of war they provided the officer corps, which kept their numbers under control."

"Okay. But somehow I don't see the Masons running France for the nouveaux riches."

She waved a hand as though I had missed the whole point.

Bill finished his wine. "You didn't come here this time of night just to chew the fat. What's up?"

"I wondered if I could borrow your car for a couple of days."

"A couple of days! Why not rent one? Or is it because your pal Mullins has friends in the CRS? *A couple of days?*"

"Maybe longer," I said.

I parked in a hotel garage along Rivoli and walked six long blocks down to the Mayol. Sidewalk places were still open and crowded, mostly with youngsters packed four or five to a tiny table full of espressos and Cokes.

I stopped by the hotel bar to say nighty-night to Imrie. He hid his surprise in amusement. "Hey, you're back so soon. I didn't expect you."

"Quasimodo was too noisy. I went for a walk and caught a taxi. Where are your friends?"

"Oh, they found a party." As he gave me a sensuous smile, the bartender set a telephone at his elbow.

"Pour vous, monsieur."

Imrie picked up the receiver. *"Oui?"* He looked at his drink and managed a casual *"ici"* before hanging up.

"Have you been invited to join the party?"

"Sure, sure. But I'm going to call it a night." He slid off the stool. "We'll see each other tomorrow—later today—all right?"

"All right."

He walked me to the elevator, and as the cage ascended I watched him strut out the main door.

When I turned on the light in my room, the chamber was undisturbed. The Econo Guide was just as I had left it.

21

THE BREAKFAST MEETING WITH PRINCE RICARD DE BORA
was dreary. He was an unmemorable man of middle
age and timid habits whose thin gray hair and wire
spectacles made him look bookish and inconsequen-
tial. His suit and skin both shared the washed-out
pallor of his eyes. I looked for relief out the window,
where rain hammered the square.

The three of us sat in a corner that the waiters
visited every fifteen minutes. As de Bora seemed
reticent, Raab did most of the talking. They flowed
from French to Italian and back, which left me able to
concentrate on my poached eggs. For the sake of
appearances, I tried once in a while to look as though I
felt left out.

Mullins hadn't shown. Neither had Greg Lord,
unless he had gotten better at hiding under tea carts.

The girls were snug in their room.

I hoped the weather would clear by one-thirty.

"Monsieur McCarry believes communications
properties are overvalued," Raab said, slipping into
English.

I didn't remember saying that, but I nodded. "Yes,
overvalued."

De Bora looked at me with no more interest than he
would have paid to the pronouncements of a coffee-
pot. He murmured in Italian to Raab, and they were
off again. It occurred to me that Raab was one of those
businessmen who found it useful to have a pet dog

sitting nearby to yap on cue. I hoped I had performed as expected.

At eleven o'clock the meeting broke up, and we saw de Bora out to a limousine under the porte cochere. As we crossed the lobby, Raab hugged a wad of papers to his belly. "Well, Donald! Prince Ricard seemed most impressed with you!" He could barely contain himself.

I played it straight. "I didn't seem to be of much use to you."

"Of course you were! By the way, do you know a man named Terrence Lippert? A magazine writer?"

"I know him slightly. Why?"

"He has been telephoning my staff in New York, demanding an interview with me for some article he is composing."

"Do you plan to grant the interview?"

"I cannot understand why I should."

The elevator let us off. Old Henri was on duty, carting valises for the oppressors.

At my door, Raab said, "Now you are at leisure. Perhaps we could consult in my chamber at four—let us say four-thirty. Your role this afternoon with Monsieur Gaubert will be more active. He is intensely interested in the mechanics of the American markets."

"I'll look forward to it." Gaubert was a new name.

"And between now and then? It is a bit drab for sight-seeing."

"I may brave the weather," I said.

"What about your pretty friends?"

"They're annoyed about last night. I slipped off to a disco without them."

He giggled as if that were the funniest trick ever played.

I went into my room and picked up the phone. When Stacy answered, I said, "One-thirty. The catty-corner building with the arches. Agreed?"

"Yes. If you really believe—"

"Don't bring anything but your passports and money. Not even an umbrella."

"All right."

"And don't open your door until you leave."

"We won't."

I kept a lookout for Mullins, Imrie, and friends on the way out of the Mayol. When a squat blue taxi pulled up, I announced my destination—"the Beaubourg"—loud enough for the front desk to hear.

Another taxi got me from the museum over to the hotel where I had dumped Bill's Fiat. With more than an hour stretching idly ahead, I settled into a café across the street. The doors were open, tables nudged against planters that separated the interior from the sidewalk. Rain kept drumming down. Traffic wove in and out at three miles an hour, bleating and bumping over the curb. A menu arrived. Ordering by dead reckoning, I got a grilled-cheese sandwich.

No Habibi, no Cha-Cha, no punk with a seven-digit bank check joined me.

At one o'clock I ducked into the hotel's garage and picked up the Fiat. The flow toward the *Opéra* was like a stopped-up bathtub. We trickled, and engines gurgled, and impatient souls tooted to make a point. Every time the rain pounded harder, the pace slowed. It was one thirty-eight when I turned into the square.

The sidewalk behind the colonnade was empty. I stopped at the curb and swabbed the passenger's window.

Water sluiced over the top of the gutter, sheeting across the sidewalk. It wasn't a very hospitable place to wait. They might have ducked into one of the shops. The nearest shop, Au Troubadour Tapis, had rugs hanging in the window.

I left the car with the engine running.

Business was slow in the carpet store. Madame

came from the back, middle-aged with gray-streaked chestnut hair and pale green eyes, and broke the language barrier. "May I help you?"

"I was supposed to meet my friends outside your shop. Two young women."

She tilted her head. "I see they are not there."

"I see too."

"You don't look like a jilted husband. A blond man came and they left with him."

"How long ago?"

She consulted a watch. "Fifteen minutes? It was endearing. He commanded and they obeyed."

"Did he have a car?"

"A red Renault."

I took Bill's car down side streets until I found enough room to park between dented vans. When I walked into the Mayol, my shoes were squishing. In the lobby, Greg Lord levered himself off a sofa. Stepping briskly, a newspaper under his arm, he paced along beside me and snapped, "What kind of game are you up to?"

"Get lost."

"You need me."

"I don't need you." Turning, I spoke loudly for anyone near the elevator. "I don't even *like* American *spies*. So piss off."

He let me ride the elevator alone.

I tried the girls' room with no response, then hammered on Mullins's door without the slightest idea what I would do if he answered. He didn't. Neither did Raab. I unlocked the door to my own room and went in. Maybe it was the haute cuisine. My bowels felt loose.

When I switched on the bathroom light and saw the room's contents, my stomach lurched, bucked, and turned itself inside out. The grilled cheese spattered into the nearest unoccupied basin, a bidet. I stood there wheezing, then twisted the faucets of the sink and ducked my head. After that I could look.

Terrence Lippert sat in the bathtub. Feet over the edge, wrists between his knees, back against the tiled wall, head sideways, frizzled hair looking as if he had spent an hour with a teasing comb or had gotten the shock of his life. It was possible. He wore a peppery Irish-tweed jacket with flecks of blue and red, flannels, expertly polished shoes, a button-down shirt. His necktie's original color was anybody's guess. The cuffs told me the shirt had been white. Last time I had seen Lippert, a pipe bowl had peeked from his breast pocket. Not now. I couldn't guess what had happened to his throat. Much of it was gone.

The tub and surrounding tiles were pristine. The mess on the shirt looked dry. Reluctantly I touched the side of one shoe, pushed. The ankle resisted, which told me only that Terrence had gotten a little stiff.

Backing out of the bathroom, I bumped into the door, opened it, and shuffled into the hall. Deep-breath time.

Having a feel for Mullins's sense of humor, I wondered if a tweedy pocket concealed a note accusing me. For the moment, I couldn't bear the thought of checking. There was one good bet. The joke wouldn't have a kick unless the police arrived. From what I had read about the Napoleonic code, a man discovered with a corpse in his bathtub could explain for a long time before being set free. If the police had an interest in pleasing a prominent person, the explanations might never prove adequate.

I walked quietly past the door to Mullins's room, past the girls', and tried the knob at Raab's suite. It was locked. So was Mullins's door.

I went back to my room. With the right attitude, you can search a dead man. Pockets are pockets, regardless of what wears them. Rusty messes are rusty messes. Pungent smells mean you don't breathe as often. All the pockets of Terrence's jacket were empty: not a billfold, not a wad of folded copy paper for note-taking, not a parking stub. I patted the trouser pockets from the outside and let it go at that. *Investor's Week*'s poison pen had become a Jacques Doe.

I opened the double doors to the balcony. It wasn't much to stand on: a wrought-iron basket perched on top of the capped columns rising from the floor below. The railing projected about eighteen inches from the wall, came to mid-thigh, and extended a foot on either side of the doors. That left a gap of about three feet between one iron basket and another.

Rain blew in my face, collected on the worn marble tiles outside. The rail was slippery under my palm. I looked down. A few cars scooted through the square. No pedestrians were on hand to watch a tourist act crazy.

I stepped over the basket and found a foothold between iron uprights on the outside. Brought the other leg over, trying not to imagine five stories of empty space. Letting go of the rail, I made a lunge.

When I slipped, it was on the shiny tiles outside Bruno Mullins's room. Crunched into the tight space, hip aching, I stared into the unlighted room. I pushed on the doors but there was no give.

Two tentative jabs of an elbow against glass left me still kneeling in the rain. I pulled back, imagining Mullins's neck, and jabbed again. The pane disintegrated. If Mullins had been napping, he was awake now.

I unlatched the doors and pushed into the room, leaving soggy footprints. The bed was made and there was no sign of clothing or luggage. I opened the door to the hall, left it ajar, and went back to my own room.

Then it occurred to me that I needed a blanket or

shower curtain. Not one from my room. I returned and collected the brocaded spread from the bed in Bruno's chamber.

Wrapping Terrence was ugly and awkward. He was stiff, not like a board but like a mechanical toy whose joints hadn't been oiled. Once there was a corner of the bedspread draped over his face, I wrestled him out of the tub. Rolled him once on the floor like a cigar getting its wrapper.

It took less than thirty seconds to drag the bundle by the heels into the neighboring room. I got it as far as the bathroom's ivory tiles. With the door closed, it might stay there until the next guest needed to use the head.

I went back and packed in less than five minutes and left the key on the dresser.

I knew exactly where to go.

Away. Fast.

That clear realism got me as far as the car. With rain sliding down my neck, I stared at the white Fiat. It wouldn't do. Just wouldn't. No matter how eager I was to get across a border.

If going away wouldn't do, then what would?

I walked west, an interminable walk, and found a handbill-adorned doorway I liked. The lobby of the two-star hotel smelled of garlic and beer. An Arab woman took two hundred francs in advance and let me find my way up to a room at the front of the third floor. I toweled off, hung up my jacket to dry. Downstairs was a pay phone. Greg Lord's room at the Mayol answered immediately.

"Mullins has Charlie's daughters," I said.

"I know that."

"What are you going to do about it?"

The line was silent.

"What I'm thinking of doing," I said, "is hunting up one of the TV bureau men over here—or maybe somebody from the *Times*—and describing how a government tax collector lets U.S. citizens get kidnapped."

"That would be stupid."

"But not up to speed with your work."

"Listen—" In mid-breath he became conciliatory. "We've got this under control. The girls are useful to Raab only to keep you in line. So they're in no real danger. Besides, I know where they're stashed."

"Where?"

"Are you ready to work with me on this?"

"All over the place. Where?"

"Let's have some tit for tat. You're not calling from the hotel—your room's empty. Where are you?"

"At a coffee shop. Public places seemed a good idea."

"Let's get together away from here," he said. "Somebody told me about a bar on the Right Bank, the Rendezvous des Amis. Can you be there at six?"

"All right." I hesitated. "By the way, Mullins left me a present. A magazine writer named Lippert. I transferred it to Mullins's room."

"What condition was the present in?"

"Not quite as bad as Roxbury Parker."

He cleared his throat. "That might be useful. I'll call the police and report gunshots in the room."

Even if the police looked at the broken window and suspected the body had been dumped, they would want to talk to Bruno. If they got clever and decided somebody had come in through the window, they might want to talk to me as well. My soggy tracks on the carpet might have dried, but there would be incriminating traces in the bathtub.

Imrie de Wohl didn't show up for the three o'clock appointment with his broker. I hung around the Ritz's Directoire lobby for ten minutes. The early afternoon crowd was the leftovers, people who hadn't breezed

160

out the door at nine A.M. looking elegant. A tall couple with matching white manes pranced off the elevator, each wearing leather coats trimmed with albino mink neckpieces, each chained to an Afghan hound that high-stepped ahead. Trying hard, but no heads turned.

The house phones were on ornamental tables decked out in mahogany and gold, with minor gods' faces on the knees, just like the Romans would have had if they hired pretentious French decorators. I asked for Monsieur de Wohl's suite and was told I meant Madame de Wohl. How silly of me.

She answered and I reminded her we had spoken when she was in London. "Oh yes, yes, Imrie's stockbroker." She had a pleasant voice with an accent I couldn't place, maybe Dutch or Belgian. "I'm afraid you missed him. If you plan to be at your office, I could have him call—I guess it's still morning in New York?"

"I guess. But I'm downstairs. Your son was going to meet me at three to review his portfolio."

"Oh, how thoughtless of him! He's out shopping. Why don't you come up and wait? It's room twelve thirty-one."

Imrie's mother was a well-preserved little bird in her fifties, with perfectly coiffed red hair and a small, sharp nose. She didn't bother pricing me after the first delicate glance. Whatever Monsieur McCarry added up to wasn't worth counting. At a guess, her flowered pink-and-green silk dress wasn't a salon knockoff but the real thing. Her jewelry was simple: an emerald ring that would have broken a maharaja's heart and a pear-shaped diamond at the base of her throat. Just the everyday stuff.

"Imrie should return in a few minutes, once he has exhausted his allowance," she said.

The reception room opened into a large living room with ceiling-high windows that seemed to pull light in from the street. Outdoors was gloomy, waiting for the next shower, but the apartment felt bright. One of the perks of spending a grand a day for a bed.

"When you called at our London place, you said something about travel business with my son." She smiled sweetly.

"I must have said I was buying travel-related investments for him. He told you he asked me to handle a little bit of money?" I had that right, at least. Two million wouldn't go far in this family. "We bought shares in a cruise line and some Disney."

"I see. He does not tell me much about his investments. Personally, I find it all very boring. But have his stocks been profitable?"

I nodded. "We've been lucky."

"Then Imrie will be delighted." That brought the chat to a natural dead end. She slipped onto another track. "Are you in Paris especially to visit clients?"

"Yes, but not all the clients are mine. A financial adviser named Raab has people he wanted me to meet."

"Why, then you should be meeting me!—if Gustav thinks I am important enough. That must be how Imrie came to you, on Gustav's recommendation?"

I didn't think the little jerk had pulled my name out of a hat. "I believe so."

"Then you should be flattered. Gustav awards few referrals. He says it takes a lifetime to know whether you can trust another. That would preclude new friendships, wouldn't it?"

"You must have known Herr Raab less than a lifetime," I said.

"No, much longer. My father did business with his father. So our knowledge traces to before the womb."

"Was that in Paris?"

"In Brussels. My father dealt with Gustav's father and uncle. The Raabs were on the bourse—before the war, of course—and had many important clients. When it became apparent that Europe would have a second war, the Raabs moved to Paris, buying time, I suppose." She lifted her shoulders delicately. "We were not so foresightful. In truth, it would not have mattered. Our family owned manufacturing plants which could not be relocated. Did you perhaps hear of Vasch Linen?"

I shook my head.

"You must have. It was one of the most famous textile producers on the Continent. That was my maiden name, Vasch. When the political climate deteriorated, we managed to sell part of our assets for unblocked currency." Her face brightened as the story improved. "Gustav's family preserved some of our capital through all that followed. So you see, I am much his admirer."

If they had preserved capital in Paris, they must have reached some accommodation with the Nazis. I phrased the thought diplomatically. "I've read that things got pretty rough in France during the war. How did you protect your money?"

"Paris was a way station. By the time of hostilities, Gustav's father and uncle had found investments in other parts of the world. I couldn't keep track— something in Spain, something else in the Argentine. Now we even have a small nonvoting interest in the Peninsula Bank."

The name rang a dim bell. "Where is that?"

"In Singapore—isn't it?"

"That sounds right."

She nodded happily. "I don't know what's keeping Imrie. Would you like a sherry or something while we wait? Now that I've told you all about our family's affairs, you must do the same."

"It's less interesting," I said.

"Was your father a stockbroker?"

"He handled other sorts of investments," I said. A punchboard was an investment.

"But you learned about finance from him?"

163

Jackie McCarry's wisdom: Never trust a check, write lots of them. "Yes, quite a lot, really."

I moved to the edge of my seat as the hallway door clicked open. Soft footsteps closed on the back of my chair. A young voice exploded: "Oh, shit! I mean, *shit!*"

I looked around.

Imrie de Wohl's pinched forehead almost disappeared in his consternation. "I stood you up, didn't I? Three o'clock, we said." He tossed an Hermès bag at the sofa and consulted a watch that had every gadget but an aircraft beacon. "Yipes, it's almost four."

"That's all right. Your mother and I have been talking."

"She's a good kid, isn't she? Did she tell you I don't know diddly about money?" His attention flitted between us.

"No, she didn't."

"Mr. McCarry has good news about your portfolio, Imrie."

He pulled a chair close, straddled it. "So we're up how much?"

"Ten percent," I said. A nice round number. But so was twenty. I wondered why I hadn't said twenty.

"You've only had the money a month. That's great. At this rate, let's see, in a year you'll have turned two million into, uh, four or five?" For a kid without a nose for money, it was a good guess. His dark eyes looked expectant, as if I might have a secret that would speed the accumulation.

One of us was having the other on. I wasn't sure which. From an old British-born colleague, who had gotten along for a quarter century on pompous grunts, I summoned my best down-to-earth manner. "Actually it would be six million and change. But we can't expect to keep compounding at this pace," I said.

"Why not?"

Because we hadn't even started? Because the best any of my clients earned in a year was twenty percent? "Well, because if anyone could make money grow at ten percent a month consistently, he would soon have all the world's money. Setbacks are inevitable."

Imrie considered that. His disappointment vanished in a moment. "So, then, the sensible thing to do is quit while I'm ahead. I mean, while you're ahead. Switch my boodle to a broker who hasn't made ten percent for a while. Let him run my stake up for a couple of months. Then switch again. It sounds cruel, I know, dumping you after you've made me a bit—"

"It sounds rude and ungrateful," his mother said.

"Besides, it wouldn't work," I said. "Your new broker might lose you twenty percent. It's a lot easier for a broker to make six mistakes in a row—or eight or ten—than to win that regularly."

"Major perverse. Can't we come up with a way to fix that? Develop an expert system program. See, you would look back on what worked for you and what didn't. Put the things that worked into the program as do's. Figure out your mistakes and write them in as don'ts. Then anytime you've got a possible investment, the expert system weighs the do's and don'ts and tells you which way to go."

"People have tried it. The problem is that things change in the market. Yesterday's *do* becomes tomorrow's *don't*, then switches back again. You've got no way of knowing which rules are working today."

His full lips formed a circle. "You're destroying my illusions, mate. So tell me about my stocks."

"First, help me out. Tell me about Gustav Raab."

"You're working for him—what can I tell you?"

"Whatever you know."

"He's a hoot."

"He gave you my name?"

"Sure, with Gustav's standard rap not to let on I

knew him." He crossed his legs and let his penny loafer dangle from a bare toe. "He said we should be able to compare notes on you—see whether you were singing the same song for both of us. Hope you're not pissed. I'd hate for us to break up if my next broker is going to lose me a bundle."

"Did Raab ask you to keep an eye on me over here?"

"Sort of. He said you were having trouble with some people. It would be good if you and your fiancée weren't running around on your own."

His stare was innocent, and I believed him.

"And you recruited your friends Habibi and Cha-Cha?" I asked.

"They're no friends of mine. Gustav knows them—though I don't know how. Cha-Cha lives down on a bleeding barge near the Eiffel Tower. He took me there the other night for some heavy partying. Gustav said they could help me. But Cha-Cha sort of takes over. Before long I was helping them." He smiled sourly. "Imrie's got no leadership qualities, that's what my old man used to say. Right, Mum?"

"He loved you despite your shortcomings."

"So—uh, are you going to tell me about my stocks?"

22

THE CLIENTELE AT THE RENDEZVOUS DES AMIS, MALE AND female, seemed to have an eye for *amis* of the same sex. It was quarter past six when I found Greg Lord at the bar, his crew cut drawing admiring glances. It had taken me two passes off Rivoli to discover that the street with the grand name rue St. Croix de la Bretonnerie was an alley wide enough for two bicycles or one drunk. Then I almost passed the bar after a glance in the window—a curtained-off diorama of small fig trees inhabited by a half-dozen lovebirds— suggested a pet store. Inside, more birds chittered in brass cages suspended from the ceiling.

Lord put his drink on the bar with a click. "Let's go for a walk."

"This place is charming."

"I'll buy you a lovebird to go." He paid the bill and we were back on the street. It was a quiet hour, too late for the Félix Potins to be getting much business. Too early for the neighborhood restaurants to have done more than hang the menu out.

He turned right at the first side street, an angled cleft between leaning limestone buildings. "What did you do that got them so nervous?" he demanded. "Nobody has come back to the hotel."

"We were planning to duck out this afternoon."

"That was stupid. I could have gotten Stacy and Beth out any time we wanted."

"Betsy," I said. "Stacy and Betsy."

"I call her Beth. You may not remember, but I've known her for years. Charlie Kimball is a friend of mine—a friend of mine and of the Treasury Department. I wouldn't let him down."

I didn't answer.

He was walking without seeming purpose. "Who have you and Raab met with?"

"There was an old man named Kostelanetz. A middle-aged prince named Ricard de Bora. We had another fellow lined up for this afternoon, which I skipped. And my client Imrie."

"Is there anything you've noticed about them?"

I thought about Kostelanetz's deep musings on diamonds, Prince Ricard's media deal, whatever it was. Young Imrie and his mum. "Dim bulbs. They've got no real understanding of finance but some pretensions. I could have sold them half of DeLorean Motors."

"They can't be too dumb if they've got money," Lord said. "What else? Is there a sign of common nationality?"

"I don't think so. Kostelanetz is from somewhere in the East, maybe Hungary. Prince Ricard is Italian, at least on one side of the family. The de Wohls were from Belgium. If they've got a common link, it's that they're all of mixed nationalities or backgrounds, sort of European crossbreeds. Kostelanetz talks like Raab, concerned about public plunder of private treasure—his own, at any rate. Raab told him they didn't have more than ten or fifteen percent of their assets in any country. Imrie de Wohl's family lost a lot of its wealth in World War Two."

"Suppose his other clients have similar histories. What then?"

"Well, it would explain Raab's appeal," I said. "You know—broad diversification, not too much vulnerability to the political climate in any region. But so what? Other people have been preaching globalization for years. To a point it makes sense to spread your assets around. You can smooth out all sorts of risk, currency swings, economic cycles, regional strengths and weaknesses. It's been going on since the seventies, markets getting more international, trading stretching round the clock. Capital has become stateless, flowing where the action is."

"Without any loyalty," Lord observed.

"What loyalty should it show? You guys think every dollar in private hands is potential revenue."

"If you mean that we assess taxes, those taxes create the infrastructure the fast-buck crowd rides on. They owe something back."

"Convince people with capital, not me," I said. There was no point arguing with a Treasury man. "If it's any consolation, they pay a price for spreading out. It's hard to get good information about what's going on next door. To be in New York or London and think you know what drives business in Singapore is a risky assumption. You get blindsided fairly often."

We crossed Rivoli and Lord managed to find a still narrower passage with a series of shallowly rising steps, beyond which lay a wedge of trees and sky. He didn't seem to care about my views on international investing. I brought the ball back to the court he knew. "If people are nervous about taxes, they do their banking in Panama or the Cayman Islands. Or probably twenty other countries. They don't blow up money managers."

"Maybe it depends on how much is at stake—huh?" He stopped, shadowed jaw thrust out. "We checked out your old friend Edna Greenleaf's beneficiary. The Heuristic Society is supposed to be an educational foundation."

"So?"

"It's unusual. They've never applied for a tax exemption. They wouldn't get one if they did. They

169

don't seem to make any grants. They don't publish an annual financial statement. The thing is domiciled, you'll be happy to hear, at a lawyer's office in Tortola. That's in the Caribbean. The lawyer is a cousin of the defense minister. As far as the U.S. Treasury Department is concerned, Mrs. Greenleaf's estate dropped into a black hole. Since we never knew the original source of the money, we've come full circle."

Hands tucked into his pockets, he walked with his head down. If he had any interest in the historic alleys we were wandering through, it didn't show. He was a man of limited enthusiasms. "Once we got interested in the Heuristic Society," he said, "we started looking for other inactive foundations. We found a few thousand on the first sweep. Most are authentic, just defunct relics—little old ladies' endowments for unwed mothers that used up their assets. But a couple stood out. We think they may be first cousins to the Heuristic Society. In the last twelve months, three have gotten about forty million in bequests. When we try to track back the donors, they have a way of turning transparent."

"That's a lot of money," I said.

"We've covered only ten percent of our list. Suppose our sample is representative. Then we have four hundred million a year dropping through the cracks thanks to Raab and his friends. Probably more, because they may have other methods. Small businesses like Whittier Mortuary. A fair amount of that money is permanently underground. For our purposes, it's invisible. We don't even really know *where* it physically is, or what it earns. So we can't tax the income."

"And you can't confiscate the whole bundle."

"The government has no interest in doing that." He wasn't a great actor.

"You've debriefed me, laid your gripes on me. Now

170

get down to it," I said. "Where are your best friend's daughters?"

"I'm taking you to them. Raab has an apartment on Île Saint-Louis. Mullins is there with the girls. We've got a covert guy from the embassy keeping an eye on them."

"Are they all right?"

"They were forty minutes ago. I left our duck blind to meet you."

We crossed the river via Pont Marie. Île Saint-Louis was an ancient part of town where cars parked with two wheels up on pinched sidewalks. Apartment buildings and hotels caught yellow streaks of sunlight in upper windows.

Lord paused at a building narrower than the others, two windows wide and lacking ornaments except for a balcony on the fourth floor. "Our listening post," he said.

"Where is Mullins?"

"Across the street, a few doors down. Let's not hang around. We'll see what Jock's got." There was an elevator midway down the hall. We got off on the third floor, and Lord led the way to an apartment at the back.

"How can your man watch things from the rear?" I said.

"Electronics."

He knocked lightly, put his face close to the door and called out, "Friends, Jock."

The man who opened the door held an automatic pistol. He looked as though he had gone to the same academy as Lord. His blond hair was cut to the sunburned scalp. His face was square and small-mouthed. He wore a blue-striped shirt with a loose burgundy foulard tie, the trousers of a tan poplin suit, tasseled cordovan loafers. If he was a Frenchman, his camouflage as a Yank was perfect.

171

"Jock, this is our troublesome friend."

"Step right in, buddy." Really covert. The Texas drawl would have fooled anyone.

I nodded to Lord. "Nobody would guess he's an American."

"McCarry's full of laughs," Lord said, closing the door. "If he wears thin, you can gag him."

The tiny mouth didn't smile. "We'll get along okay. My buddy and me'll have a coupl'a Coronas and talk football. You like football?"

Around him the room was a clutter of half-eaten meals and cases of beer. Light came from a high-wattage overhead fixture. Both windows wore closed shutters and half-drawn draperies.

"How long do I have to baby-sit?" he asked.

"Just till I get things squared away. If I haven't turned up Raab and his friends in forty-eight hours, we may as well go home." Lord glanced around the room, looking neither shocked nor disgusted but faintly nostalgic, as if his favorite years had been spent with week-old dinner plates. "I don't want this clown running around compromising everything I do. McCarry, you be a good boy."

"Do you have any idea what you're doing?" I said.

"Yeah. First I put the Paris cops on to Mullins. Then, if he and Raab get picked up together, I pull strings and get Raab peeled off for myself. If I can get a look at his papers, we identify the clients and go after them. We may not get our host country to cooperate on that part. But I'll tell you this—any assets this bunch has within the borders of the U.S. they can kiss good-bye."

He hadn't mentioned getting the girls back.

"A more likely scenario," I said, "is that Raab pulls strings and you get fished out of the Seine. If Mullins could get the security police to jump at the airport, he's got connections. Then there's another problem. You don't know where Raab is. I do."

Lord stared at me. "Bullshit. You came here like a puppy dog on a leash. You don't know a thing."

"When we came over, I didn't know I knew. I hadn't had time to digest something. Now I have."

The creases around his mouth deepened. He told Jock: "Our friend's a stockbroker. He's got a talent for scooping it on deep and thick. For my money, you can handcuff him to the bed for the next two days."

"They're on a barge," I said quickly. "I know where."

"How would you know that?"

"I was told—indirectly. It didn't register at first. Now it's the only thing that makes sense."

He folded his arms and gave me the stare government reserves for unruly citizens. "Why a barge? Why not a rowboat? Why not the Eiffel Tower?"

"A barge is more convenient. One of Raab's goons is from a family that lives on a river barge."

"That could be true," Jock said. "There's thousands of those people. Sort of clannish water gypsies. They're called *bateliers.*"

"I don't give a fuck what they're called," Lord said.

"I know where the barge Raab's using is berthed," I said. Before he could utter his next demand, I added, "I'll show you."

23

DOWN ON THE QUAY, A MAN IN A DIRTY SWEATER AND JEANS threw a can clattering across the paving blocks. Three dogs yammered in pursuit, and their battle for possession chased the can from the quay's edge to a line of poplars that rose beside the fortresslike stone wall that stretched along the river. Peering through branches from atop the wall, the avenue behind him, Greg Lord puffed on a cigar and pretended to enjoy the evening view. It hadn't rained in more than an hour. Nearby, traffic streamed across Pont d'Iéna to the Left Bank.

He blew out smoke. "Which barge?"

They lay at hundred-foot intervals for as far in either direction as I could see. Fortunately an industrial area occupied the opposite side of the river, so we only had to inspect every boat on this shore. I wished Imrie had been more specific. Just a bleeding barge down near the Eiffel Tower. The tower loomed on the far bank a half-mile downstream.

"One of them," I said.

Lord's friend from the embassy, Jock Mizel, had gone for a stroll. He came back shaking his head. "There's a ramp down to the quay a little way up the road and a stairway that goes down near the bridge. It's impossible to keep every access under surveillance."

"He doesn't know which barge," Lord said.

Mizel leaned against the top of the wall, peering down. "It probably ain't these folks below us."

The can tosser had sprinted up a gangway. On the long, flat cabin roof, edged with pots of flowers, a table stood draped in a white cloth. Two women set out plates and glasses while a boy carried a wine bottle close to his chest. Near the bow a lantern cast a yellow balm on the scene.

The next barge had laundry hanging from a line stretched between radio masts. A two-toned Citroen was parked on the deckhouse. An old man was dozing in a sling chair on the front deck.

Walking along the wall, we inspected a dozen other barges. A couple looked possible—closed-up vessels with nobody in sight. Most appeared convincingly benign.

"Even if you heard right, they could have cast off," Mizel said.

From the islands of rubbish collected around each barge, I didn't think they left often. "Let's check out a couple of possibles," I said.

"Wait a min. Your buddy said near the Eiffel Tower. Let's take a walk downriver."

We walked a quarter of a mile, and I spotted Habibi. He was loping down a ramp from the avenue, a duffel bag slung over one shoulder. He wore grubby chinos and a turtleneck shirt that flapped loose at the waist. With no sign of concern about being followed, he turned upriver and ran up the gangway of a barge that looked like a floating bicycle shop. Bicycles and parts of bicycles were stacked on the low cabin roof. Chassis sections littered the decks. Expensive-looking racing bikes hung from hooks on the deckhouse. On a bare corner of the pilothouse roof, Bruno Mullins sat in khakis and a tank shirt, taking the evening air.

"Well, well," said Greg Lord.

"So what's next?" Mizel asked. "Do we gallop to the rescue?"

"We don't know if Raab is there. I need Raab."

Drifting away from them, I started toward the narrow ramp that connected the avenue to the quay. When I was five steps from it, Greg Lord called, "Come back here!"

I went down the slippery paving at a trot. The quay was empty except for a strolling couple who passed me absorbed in themselves. The man's beret was pulled down to his eyebrows. A bony hand clutching a cigarette wove a pretty picture in the air.

Mullins was barely visible through the hardware. I approached the gangway and called his name.

He came around fast, hurling himself flat on the

roof. A short-barreled machine pistol peeked over the edge and zeroed in on my chest. His eyes swept the quay. Peripherally I saw Lord and Mizel reach the bottom of the ramp and head in the opposite direction. They pretended to be in no hurry.

I held my hands away from my sides. "Easy, Bruno. You don't want to bring every cop in Paris."

He didn't answer. Didn't shoot, either.

I tried again. "That package you left for me—I dumped it back in your room."

His attention shifted to the trees and the top of the wall. He wriggled across the roof, slid his legs over the edge, and dropped to the deck in a crouch. If he had a knife in his garter belt, he was getting into throwing range. He beckoned with a finger. "Come onto the deck."

I stayed put. "Raab and I need to talk."

"Come aboard, you talk."

"You're too impulsive, Bruno. Ask your boss to come on deck. He'll want to hear what I have to say before you blast me."

"That's most unlikely. But you need not fear for your immediate health. If I wished, you would die silently at this moment."

"Then my friends would turn impulsive. They have you surrounded."

He chuckled. "The authorities would never permit you to approach if they were here."

From behind him, out of sight, a voice hissed. "Bruno, bring the boy inside! I do wish to speak with him!" A bit louder: "You have my assurance, my dear boy. This is all a most dreadful misunderstanding."

"No problem." Arms folded, I pivoted and swept a quick look along the quay. The place was deserted. No problem. I shouted: "Your Nazi has made things awkward!"

"Eet can all be worked out!"

176

Yez, indeedy.

I went up the gangway, stepped onto the deck. A scabrous pink bicycle separated me from Mullins, who crouched below the gunwale in case I really did have a sharpshooter in reserve. He held a knife with a straight serrated blade in his left hand, casually bouncing it for balance. He nodded me past him.

He followed me to the rear deck, duck walking. Something caught my foot and I stumbled. He was on me in an instant, pressing the blade against my spine. "Get up. Go."

The door was dogged back. The interior, beyond the first two descending steps, was hidden in darkness. Mullins punched the middle of my back.

"Get your hand off," I said.

Something rose up from the deck and slammed my head. Maybe an anchor. My skull banged the lintel and I fell into the empty blackness.

The headache filled the world except for a cup of tea steaming under my nose. Betsy Kimball sat on a divan in a cramped, filthy cabin, holding a cracked mug. She had her hair tied into a bun, implausibly prim, and her legs tucked under her. Her white shorts and blouse were grubby. So were her knees and elbows. She pulled the tea away. "They let me make this for you. If you don't want it, that's okay. It covers up how bad things smell in here." She sniffed. "Including me."

I sat up slowly, glad—more glad than I could have guessed—to see that immature face. Not that I'd gotten her into this fix—that was her own fault, or Stacy's, or Greg Lord's, or Charlie Kimball's. If I worked on it a while, I could fasten the blame on Imrie. But I was glad to see her.

"Stacy's in our cabin." She whispered. "We goofed up. Bruno knew when we left. And there he was, just like at the airport."

177

"Has anyone been, uh, hurt?"

"If it weren't for Mr. Raab it would get hairy. He's a restraining influence. Here. You may as well drink this. Your head's bloody, you know."

Above the ear I felt a clump of matted hair. Most of the skull was in place. "Who else is aboard?"

"Those two boys, Cha-Cha and Habibi—because the boat belongs to Cha-Cha's uncle or something. The uncle stays in a room up back under the bridge or whatever you call it. Mr. Raab has a little cabin. And you know about Bruno. He was trying to ask us questions just before you came—Bruno, with Mr. Raab watching."

"What questions?"

"Who you were working for. How much did you know. Was the U.S. government going to attach Raab Capital's assets. Like we would know."

Your father might, I thought. I listened to the silence in the cabin. The barge was old, built solid with heavy wood walls and doors that wore generations of lumpy paint. The fact I couldn't hear anything on the rest of the boat didn't mean nothing was going on.

"How long was I unconscious?"

"At least an hour."

"When I've had my tea, will they take you back to Stacy?"

"I don't know."

"Bang on the door and let's find out. If it works, tell your sister that at the first sign of trouble you two should climb under the bunk. Lie low. There may be shooting." There almost certainly would be shooting. Lord and Mizel would be coming. We might have only minutes. "Go on, sweetheart."

She stood up with a tentative smile. "The tea isn't a big hit, huh?"

I took the mug. The stuff was strong and bitter. "It's just what I want."

She smiled and went to hammer on the door. "Let me out of here!"

Cha-Cha opened the door, dark face suspicious.

"Let me out!" she cried. "He's a total pig! I want to go back to my sister. Anywhere but here!"

He smiled faintly, saluted me with two fingers. "Sure thing. My cabin's free."

"Let it stay that way." She pushed past him.

Cha-Cha stuck out his tongue at me. "Boss wants to see you. Stand up and stuff your hands in your pockets."

He pulled a small, rough-edged automatic out of his hip pocket and tossed it from hand to hand. His eyes didn't bother following the transits. "Hey, you think you can take me while I'm fuckin' around?"

"Did Raab ask you to fuck around?"

"C'mon, smart ass."

We shuffled down a passageway made narrower by an extraordinary clutter piled against the walls, a world-class bazaar of scrap bicycle parts. Up a short flight of stairs, I used my shoulder to push open a door and stepped into the pilothouse. Gustav Raab reclined on a floral couch. The room was brightly lit. Its windows gave back our reflections over glimpses of a darkened quay. From the top of the wall we must present tempting targets. It should have made me nervous. Lord couldn't do much that came out right.

Raab waved a languid hand at the pilot's chair. "Sit, my dear boy. It will be small comfort to you, but I blame myself most severely for this misfortune. When we suspected you had betrayed our confidence, we could merely have severed the tie without unpleasantries. Instead, curiosity took hold. We became like the ferocious little terrier with an old carpet slipper, shaking it, growling, fussing."

"Very well put," I said. I perched on the swivel stool, pulled my feet up. Mullins was a darling terrier.

The Kewpie-doll face with the painted goatee widened in pleasure. "Well, but you see now the problem is acute. You have friends stalking us. We really must know who they are and what they know."

Cha-Cha had gone over to stand by the window, holding the pistol out of sight under an arm.

"Not to be critical," I said, "but if you don't know those things, Mullins is providing poor security."

"Bruno does not provide security. He is more—I guess the American equivalent would be chief auditor. I told you he trained at a Swiss bank."

"He was too young for the SS?"

"He might have excelled in a number of callings. Bruno's rough exterior is an asset, because it seldom occurs to people that his first talent is finance."

I accepted that with a blank face. Because I *knew* what Bruno's first talent was.

Raab wagged pudgy fingers at nothing. "Younger people, such as Monsieur Bouvoir here"—he nodded at Cha-Cha—"are more appropriate for security, more enthusiastic. Like many of his fellow nationals, Cha-Cha is a revolutionary. He knows nothing of the organization to which he hires out his gun. It does not matter to him, or us, that he would oversee our execution if his comrades ever came to power—which shall never happen, of course. For the time being, we have a liaison of convenience."

"Perhaps he's taking names. Does he knit in the evenings?"

"You enjoy your jests. No, no—we know much more of Cha-Cha than he knows of us. He is giving you a dirty look, Donald. Your remark of knitting he interprets as an insinuation of femininity."

"I'm sorry that he's sensitive on the point."

Raab shrugged. "Why be sensitive? One does what entertains one, yes? But we must concentrate on business. Your friends—there was a man at the hotel clearly in the employ of some governmental department. One recognizes the mix of petty authority and narrow intelligence. Who is he?"

"His name is Greg Lord."

"For whom does he work?"

"The U.S. Treasury, I believe."

"And the man whose car you drove?"

"He's not involved."

"No?"

"He's just a friend."

"We have a name—Hinsdale."

"He's not with the government." My collar was suddenly soggy, and my sides felt hot. "He's a stockbroker. We knew each other at Columbia. He gave me the tip on Electronics Corporation of Belgium. You made a lot of money on that."

"You needn't go on, Donald. It is enough that he does not work for the government. Almost certainly enough. You told him nothing?"

"Nothing."

Tiny lips pursed. "Now you are being untruthful. Certain inquiries came back to me, which Mr. Hinsdale had made."

"He knows you're a client of mine. I asked him to check your reputation over here."

"And?"

"And your firm likes to promote an image of exclusivity. That's all."

"I was merely curious. Very well. Will it please you if we forget Monsieur Hinsdale and his family?"

I swallowed. "Yes."

"It is done."

I tried to take a breath.

"So then we have Monsieur Terrence Lippert, journalist, deceased. He was most persistent. Yet upon being questioned, he knew nothing. Certainly nothing damaging to our interests. Is it possible he was so ignorant?"

My head was swimming. Where were Greg Lord and the cavalry?

"Is that possible?" Raab said. "That he truly knew nothing?"

"He was a magazine writer. It's almost a certainty."

"He had conferred with you."

"I didn't confer with him. I used him once. I fed him a story about a bond issue our firm was doing. He suspected you and I were doing business and pestered me for leads. I didn't give him any. I didn't know he was in Paris."

"He had learned from your office that you were here. My people, I am certain, were more discreet."

If they weren't he could have Mullins *audit* them.

"But to the point," Raab said. "If he knew nothing, why was he so much insistent?"

"You were just a story." My lips didn't want to move. My brain mumbled about shutting down for the evening. "Money managers are seven-day wonders in the financial press. For God's sake, don't you read *Barron's* or *Investor's Week?"*

"I do not waste my time."

"Terrence thought you would be good for an interview or two. Reporters always need new sources. You would have been a little exotic."

"But he pursued us here!"

"An expense-account vacation . . ."

He fell silent. The knowledge that they had murdered somebody for nothing wouldn't make him miss a meal. But to a fussbudget about discretion, Mullins's work must seem a clumsy, attention-grabbing excess. The Little King wasn't smiling. "So, we should not have been so concerned. I accept that. But now we come to you, my boy. What do you know?"

I couldn't look in that direction, but I wondered about the window on the side of the pilothouse opposite Cha-Cha. How thick it was. Whether a good run would carry me through. Whether Greg Lord couldn't give the green light soon to retire Cha-Cha. I met Raab's eye. "I know a bad stock when I see one. Not much else."

"You are modest. Surely if you have consorted with a Treasury Department agent, you have picked up suspicions? And you have met some Raab clients. What do you surmise?"

"You're in the business of dispersing money," I said. Not knowing quite what I meant.

He nodded politely. "True, true. Ah—Cha-Cha! It is time for your uncle to come assist us. See if all is well on deck."

The boy left. Blurred figures moved on deck. The barge seemed to shift slightly.

A grizzled man in soiled trousers and a sleeveless undershirt climbed up from belowdecks. He saw me and muttered, *"Merde!"* Waved me off the stool. Stepping close to the window, I could see two men on deck holding long poles, pushing us silently from the quay. Lights on the opposite bank were moving. Greg Lord had waited too long. We were under way.

24

THE OLD MAN STARTED THE ENGINES AS WE PASSED UNDER Pont d'Iéna.

"Uncle Hugo speaks no English," Raab said. "His nephew desires to murder him and inherit the barge.

That is not our affair. You are quite right. Raab Capital exists to deploy assets globally. What is wrong with that?"

"Nothing as far as I'm concerned. Greg Lord is pretty sure your clients don't pay their fair share of taxes. That's all right with me, too."

"And you—you imagine there is something else?"

I'd been wondering if he was going to tell me. A bad sign if he did. I said, "I haven't been wondering at all. But the Treasury people are curious. They think it might be Russian money. You know, buying up America on the qt."

"That is most amusing. The confiscators are worried about bolshevism. It would intrigue your Mr. Lord to know just how reputable our money is. It comes from aristocrats, royalty, industrialists, trading dynasties, landowners—even a few military families. Most of it is very, very old. Its owners have learned survival skills."

"Why would your lifted-pinky crowd invest in the U.S.?" I asked.

"No need to flatter yourself, Donald. We have interests in most Western economies—and in some not Western, if the rulers are not too inhospitable." He stared at his reflection and the flowing lights. "Have you wondered how there is no surviving Medici bank? The family embodied a great commercial power in the fifteenth century. Medici banks thrived in Florence, Rome, Venice, Naples, Milan, Pisa, Avignon, Geneva, Lyons, even Bruges, financing medieval trade. Yet, today, of that fortune no trace survives. Why?"

He let the question hang only for a moment. Not long enough for me to cite the mediocrity of third generations.

"The cause will be familiar to you, a very modern tragedy," Raab said. "The Medicis' affairs were inextricably linked with those of political and papal authorities. Sovereigns were prolific clients, that is to say, prolific borrowers. In particular, the duke of Burgundy regarded borrowed funds much as he viewed captured treasure, as his own by divine will and intercession. His defaults brought the Medicis to ruin.

"You might wonder about the Ariel trading house. In the seventeenth century their caravans showered goods from much of the Orient on Europe's awakening middle class—a wonder of diplomacy, given the barbaric lords who lay between. The family owned estates in the Loire that a good horseman could not circle in three days. Today the Ariels are unknown. The Revolution, in purging the ancien régime, turned over their land to peasants and seized every other vestige of their wealth in 'taxation.'

"Wealth that has survived the centuries has learned to blend in with its surroundings, Donald. Visibility excites the envy of any chance mob. So pieces are kept small, the base of assets is diversified. Intelligent wealth does not behave like the street-corner tart who says, 'Here I am, take me!' It confuses, obfuscates, muddles the footprints of identity. It buys quiet influence. And it survives the upheavals that sweep away the incautious."

I said, "A game of hide-the-ducat—is that it? How long have you been running the show?"

"I do not run it. I am a mere servant, as you were."

"Then who calls the shots?"

He spread pudgy fingers. "I do not know. Nor do I care to conjecture. It is folly to confront a Gorgon, yes? That is our little fanciful name for the asset pool we manage—Gorgon."

I remembered the article Greg Lord had showed me about the bond executive who took a dive. If I wanted to make a list I could add Robert Petrus, Roxbury Parker, Terrence Lippert. A lot of flesh turned to stone when the Gorgon felt jittery.

"Where do you wear your tattoo?" I said, thinking of Jerry's.

He smiled and didn't answer.

"This sounds like big money," I said.

"I have little concept," he said. "My father and uncle never learned its scope. There must be other managers such as myself, but I know none of them, nor their location. You understand, I make no effort —ever—to repair that ignorance."

"What about Kostelanetz and de Bora?"

"Members of the investment committee to which I report—not the most important members. These gentlemen are totally respectable. Insofar as visible wealth is concerned, each is a dutiful citizen proudly contributing to his government's upkeep."

Lippert, I thought, hadn't even been looking for the truth. He had just touched a trip wire at the perimeter, stumbling after an interview. Bad luck that a fanatic like Bruno patrolled the boundary.

I wondered how many of the happy children hanging out at Portofino cafés got monthly checks because Grandfather was paranoid. What would they say if they knew about Bruno's tidying up? Enjoying the sun, would they care much about a tweedy journalist?

"We are disappointed in you, Donald," Raab said. "We brought you very profitable business. We steered acquaintances to you. In a few years, you could have retired. Or perhaps set yourself up as an independent financial manager. Instead you conspired against us."

"I guess your idea of independence isn't mine," I said. "It would get old, having someone I couldn't see pulling my strings."

"Few people don't. You would simply know it." He had pressed a button or given some other signal. Habibi came up the companionway. "Take our friend to his cabin," Raab said. "Bruno wishes an interview later."

* * *

186

Around dawn they let me use the head. There was a small window cranked open to catch a breeze. It showed sloping stone levees topped by farmland. We moved slowly to the throb of Uncle Hugo's engines. Onshore an early riser plodded along at the crest of the embankment, arms scything with military vigor. He was abreast of us for a moment, weathered face content in the pleasure of his pipe and exercise. I watched with envy.

During the night, Greg Lord, Jock Mizel, and the cavalry hadn't arrived.

Neither had Bruno Mullins interviewed me.

As luck went, it was at least a wash.

Cha-Cha took me back to my cabin. There was no talk of breakfast. Unable to sleep, I lay on the bunk and stared at the ceiling joists.

An appearance by Greg Lord no longer seemed likely. He must have balanced pros and cons and opted for Raab and the Seine to dispose of his botched case.

At nine-thirty, the engines slowed to a deep rumble. There was a slipping feeling as the barge drifted, then a jarring bump and creaking. I guessed we had put in to shore.

Rolling off the bunk, I tried listening. There were voices, but not close. After a while I tried hammering at the door. When that didn't help I tried a few kicks.

Cha-Cha opened the door looking cross, pointing his gun about six inches below my belt. "You wanna fuck with me?"

"Not on your life. Raab said I could use the potty when I need to. I need to."

"You fuckin' got a weak bladder?"

When I looked embarrassed, he grinned and took me down to the head. Staying there long was physically impossible. The toilet must have been installed when the barge was built, fifty or sixty years ago, and had been scrubbed once every decade since. Holding my breath, I stood on tiptoe and looked out the window. We were pulled in at a stone pier, lines secured to ringbolts trailing rust streaks to the water. Quite a ways off, Mullins and Habibi were talking to someone in a black stretch Citroen that must have come across the decayed rail right-of-way where weeds grew like small trees. The limousine was parked well out on the pier's scree of broken glass. The rear window on the water side was rolled down, but Mullins's body concealed the passenger.

Bruno was tilting forward from the waist, an attentive waiter taking those martini orders. Habibi had wandered a few feet from the car. He looked back our way.

I brought down a foot on the flusher, opened the door.

Cha-Cha was leaning against a wall full of handlebars. He pulled the gun from his jeans, scratched a hairy patch of belly. "Back to your hole."

"Why are we stopped?"

"The Swiss guy is bringing on a supply of tweezers and nail files. You know what for?"

As I started down the passage, Raab appeared at the door of his cabin. He beckoned to the boy. "We wish to interrogate Mr. McCarry again. Bring him and wait outside."

Raab's cabin smelled as bad as my own. His gray double-breasted suit and silk necktie declared he was making only the necessary concessions to a *batelier*'s life. He closed the door, raised a finger to his lips. "Bruno will have questions for you and the young ladies. Not many questions. Then he will entertain himself for a few hours. Your bodies will be dumped in a gravel excavation that is near this landing."

I listened and wondered why he was being so specific.

"That is the harsh but literal truth, Mr. McCarry.

As I grow older, perhaps I am getting the weak, sentimental stomach. It pains me to imagine the ladies receiving Bruno's attention. He is a beast."

The blankets on his cot concealed a length of metal tubing, a section of frame from a bicycle that had been painted several times before getting a layer of glossy electric blue. At one end, a nickel-plated sleeve had held handlebars.

He handed the pipe to me, pointed to the wall beside the door. Flinging himself onto the bunk, he struck a cowering pose and screamed. *"Help! Help! He kills me!"*

Nothing happened. He drew a breath. *"Cha-Cha! Help!"*

The boy hurtled through the door so fast that my swing barely brushed his shoulder. He stumbled into Raab, fired muffled shots into the bedding. I swung the pipe down and missed the curly head but caught his neck. It slowed him. I hammered the knob against his wrist. He lost the gun. Twisting away, he tried rolling against my legs.

Raab snatched up the gun. He ignored Cha-Cha. He aimed the muzzle at the center of my chest and without so much as calling me "dear boy" snapped off three shots.

I couldn't tell exactly where they struck as Cha-Cha sprang up. His head jerked back, his jaw vanished in red mist, his shoulders convulsed, and his arms hugged empty air. Uncle Hugo would keep his barge. I heaved the boy onto Raab and pounded on the chubby hand until the gun came free.

His abrupt change of heart didn't surprise me as much as the temporary alliance had. One way or another, Raab wanted me unavailable for a chat with Mullins.

I peered out at the shore.

The Swiss still bent forward at the Citroen. Habibi

was grinding something under his boot. On the far side of the car a door stood open, and somebody short leaned against the roof, mostly obscured by Mullins.

Nobody seemed to have heard the gunfire.

I backed up.

Raab was pinned to the cot by the corpse. He pushed away an arm that lay across his face, and his eyes followed as I checked the corridor. I closed the door, leaned against it, examined the gun. It was a small automatic, with a gray-blue chiseled look like a tool fresh from a machine shop. There was a lever on the left that I guessed was a safety catch. A magazine in the enlarged butt that I didn't disturb.

"Where is Uncle Hugo?" I said.

"He drinks. He is asleep."

Pointing the gun at Raab's face, I pulled on Cha-Cha's arm. He came slowly, like a sleeper refusing to wake. When the balance of weight shifted, he rolled onto the floor.

"Take off your necktie and lie on your face," I said.

"If you are to escape, you will need the ally," Raab said, as he moved to the floor.

"Lie on your face." Planting a knee on his back, I bound his wrists.

"Please, you will not leave me face-to-face with this unlucky child."

I threw a towel over the unlucky child.

Then I went down the passageway. For someone who hadn't washed her face in twenty-four hours, Stacy looked just fine. The sandy hair was rumpled. The grubby shirtsleeves were rolled back. Chinos looked like she had been mud wrestling. All terrific.

She flew off the filthy bunk, her sister a step behind. She reached me with a crushing hug. "I heard shots—"

"So are we rescued?" Betsy said.

"No sign of it. But we've got a chance. Is Cha-Cha's uncle in on this?"

"I think he does what they tell him," Stacy said. "As long as they pay. Where is everybody?"

"Mullins and Habibi are all we have to worry about, and they're on shore. I'm going up to the deck. You see if there are any guns lying around. Stay out of Raab's cabin."

I went up through the forward companionway, wriggled behind a screen of bicycles. The tableau on the pier hadn't changed materially. Habibi was maybe a little farther from the barge, arms folded in a display of boredom. Mullins might have been frozen in place. The short figure from the other side of the Citroen had come around and was a woman. She was dressed in something like black harem pants and a red gypsy blouse. Even at the distance, close to a hundred yards, her pale features had a distinct Asian cast. The only time we had met, she had tried to kick my head off. Jerry the easy pickup.

Across a gap of about four feet, the barge was secured to the pier by lines fore and aft. A gangway stretched across the chasm from the aft deck, just under the pilothouse. Head below the barge's gunwale, I crept over to the nearest line. A long coil of heavy rope was woven around a buckle on the deck, then draped across to the ringbolt on the wall.

Even if I had a knife, it would take a long time to saw through the thick lines.

Ducking back to the door, I called softly. Stacy appeared, holding a rifle that Uncle Hugo might have used in the Marne. "I can't find bullets," she said.

"Never mind. Come up here."

A ten- or twelve-foot wooden pole hung on brackets above the deckhouse windows. Keeping my back to the shore, I stood up, lifted the pole down to the deck. "It's heavy. You'll have to balance it on top of the rail, then push against the pier. Once you've given a push," I said, "or if you lose the pole or see a gun over there, get below and lie flat."

"What are you going to do?"

"Untie us."

It all depended on who was looking our way. Jerry might not distinguish one scruffy, shambling man from another. Habibi or Mullins would.

I kept my chin down. Stepping between a pair of upended racing cycles, I climbed the railing and jumped to shore.

I acted like it was my business to add a few tightening loops to the ring. When the line came free, I let it slide into the water.

I was halfway down to the stern when Habibi got tired of mashing ants and turned around. When he yelled in Arabic, I waved casually. Reached the line. Bent and undid it.

Mullins understood before Jerry did. From under his arm he pulled a pistol with a disturbingly long barrel and fired a half-dozen shots that whined on the iron curb or punched through the barge walls. I ducked and ran.

Over a shoulder, I saw Jerry in motion.

It was an interesting contest. I had to cover six feet to the gangway, dump it, and jump four feet to the deck. She had to cross a hundred yards.

It was a dead heat. I was heaving the gangway off the railing when she was ten yards away. Stacy had pushed, and the gap between the barge and the shore was widening. The gangway upended and splashed.

Jerry hurtled ahead as the clamor brought Betsy onto the deck. The little panther launched itself. It was like seeing a cat levitate up a wall. Slippered feet caught the wood trim on top of the gunwale. Arms churned for balance. Betsy was close, too close, unaware of the lethal danger of those feet.

"Get away from her!"

There wasn't time.

The little panther was bending its knees, lowering the center of gravity, winning the battle to stay aboard. She was almost crouching when Betsy handed her—it wasn't quite a toss—a child's tricycle, high at shoulder level. Putting the center of gravity very far back. A foot stroked the air as her weight shifted.

I leapt across, caught the railing, and swung over, passing a few feet from Jerry, who fell into the river. "Get below," I shouted.

The deckhouse wall took on pockmarks as Mullins fired spaced shots while he ran.

The barge was drifting, very slowly. The bow responded to the current's tug while the stern resisted like a sluggish drunk clinging to a good park bench. When Mullins reached the edge of the pier, fifteen feet separated him from the barge. Too much to jump. He jammed a new magazine into his gun, leveled it, and fired a low barrage that started at the bow, where he had last seen a head; he worked aft with the deliberation of a craftsman pounding tacks.

On the sheltered side of the boat, I scrambled into the pilothouse. From the edge of the water, Habibi saw movement and devoted himself to tearing apart the windows and frames. He had a small-caliber gun but it was hell on glass and half-rotted wood. I held my arms over my head as splinters pelted down. A moment later Mullins brought heavier artillery to bear, hammering the walls. The bigger slugs smashed through. Only the angle, which gave me the floor as a partial shield and directed most of the fire overhead, made the pilothouse survivable. Even then it was impossible to do more than lie flat and let the debris accumulate.

I felt Cha-Cha's automatic in my front pocket but had no thought of returning fire.

A pause in the fusillade provided a chance for a look at the controls. There was an ignition switch but no key. That could be dealt with if I had time.

In any case, there was a more immediate problem. The barge was drifting sideways, the bow pointing—

as nearly as I could guess from the gunfire's source—almost directly at the opposite shore. Not far downstream an arm of land stretched out to snare us. If we wallowed this way for a bit longer, we would get hung up and offer a stationary target.

I grabbed the bottom spoke of the wheel, spun it hard to the right—and dropped back as someone resumed shooting.

The boat's response was grudging. Watching the sky, I saw a cloud rotate gently to the left. Which meant that the bow was swinging to the right. Not too much, I hoped, just enough to get us pulled into the current toward the center of the river.

Again the shooting stopped. Betsy called from the companionway, "Are you all right?"

"Stay down there."

"Uncle Hugo is hiding under his bed."

"Good. Keep him out of Raab's cabin." He might be sentimental about the killer nephew.

When I peered over a window ledge, we were twenty feet from shore, a hundred feet downstream from the landing. Mullins had turned his back to the river. He pushed another clip into the butt of his gun. Two men climbed out of the car. One, a tall black-haired man I didn't recognize, ran forward clutching a machine pistol. Mullins waved him aside. A clear *Don't bother.* The other figure, white-haired and ursine, was Dmitri Kostelanetz, who snapped a beckoning hand at Mullins.

One of Gorgon's eminences.

Our movement had the grace of a wallowing whale, but ahead the channel looked clear. The spit of land would pass to our right with fifty feet to spare. I steered toward the river's center for a wider margin.

There was a thump outside. I looked through the vacant door expecting to see Stacy or Betsy. I scanned the deck. For a moment nothing registered. Then, screened by dismembered cycle parts, two sets of pale-knuckled fingers shifted along the top of the gunwale, beside the aft line, which dragged through the water.

She was out of the river, raven hair slicked back, naked feet thrashing for a purchase on the narrow rim where the gunwale rose from the hull. One sleeve of the red gypsy blouse was ripped free at the shoulder, and the sodden front of the fabric clung to her small breasts. The black harem pants were drifting somewhere in the Seine. Pale thigh muscles bunched with effort.

She saw me looming overhead as I pulled Cha-Cha's gun from my pocket. She clutched with miniature toes and finally got a purchase that let her cling like a suspended frog, knees hugging her shoulders.

I pulled back the slide, making certain a cartridge was in the breech, and pointed the muzzle at the bridge of her nose. "Back in the water, babe."

She strained to lift herself, primal and determined. She gasped and managed a crooked grin. "I've just come to play."

"Go play with Bruno."

"You're no fun."

"If you don't get off this boat, I'm going to shoot you."

When she decided that I meant it—and I did, almost—an expression of forlorn, childish disappointment swept the small face. She calculated her chance of getting a foot high enough to catch me in the face. Not good.

She splashed backward into the river, came up sputtering, and pouted at me as the boat drifted past.

Stacy looked over the rail. "Who the hell is that?"

"That's Jerry. We've been dating since you left for Paris."

"She looks like the perfect girl for you, Donald."

"She has personality flaws," I said.

* * *

195

Hot-wiring the ignition took all of a minute. It turned out that the pier lay in a branch that had split from the river's main channel, a secluded spot for mayhem. A mile downstream, the two arms came together again and the traffic was heavier. As we passed a cluster of barges powering upriver together toward Paris, heads turned on the nearest decks as the *bateliers* appeared to recognize Uncle Hugo's bike emporium but not the passengers.

A bit farther downstream we passed a village where swimmers splashed near the shore. With one hand on the wheel, I dug through cluttered drawers hoping to find a chart that would tell me where we were. The old man liked *romans policiers* with bare-breasted suspects on the cover. He apparently knew the river by heart.

There would be towns and cities ahead—places where boats could be taken out to intercept us. I wondered if Mullins and his crew knew the river any better than I did.

I eased up on the throttle. Stacy said, "You look unhappy."

"We probably haven't lost our friends for long."

She glanced at the shore. "There's no road along here."

She was right. Just sun-browned fields and orchards and acres of cobalt sky waiting for an artist's muddying strokes. If a highway ran parallel to the river, it swung in close to the water only at intervals.

That was encouraging. At least they couldn't track us exactly.

I handed over the wheel and went below. Armed with a wrench, Betsy stood guard outside Uncle Hugo's scarred door. She smiled self-consciously. I entered the cabin, which smelled like an all-night wine bar at dawn. I drew the gun and prodded Uncle Hugo's sleeping belly. Coming awake with a snarl, he rolled off the cot onto his knees. He shook his head.

I backed up and beckoned with the gun. However feeble his English, his guttural outpouring's meaning jumped easily across the language barrier. A few of his gestures and suggestions had to do with the gun.

The three of us went upstairs. Stacy put an arm around his shoulders and urged him to the window. He took in the damage in a sweeping glance that seemed to accept bullet holes as a cost of business.

When Stacy asked where we were, he barely looked at the shore. *"La Seine."*

"Where is the next town? How large?"

The shrug was eloquent. How would he know?

"Ask him if he was in cahoots with Mullins."

She reported his response. "He hires the barge."

Uncle Hugo added something.

"He would even hire to a child molester such as you, Monsieur," she said.

"Offer him a thousand francs a day to take us to the mouth of the river. To Le Havre, I think. We can get something across to England."

"Don't you want to get in touch with Mr. Lord?"

I told her about Mr. Lord's priorities. She was dismayed. "My father thinks he's a *friend."* She passed my offer to Uncle Hugo. The language of his shrugs was becoming comprehensible. This one said, "Commerce is commerce."

He muttered. Stacy said, "He would like payment now, for three days."

"All right." I went below and rifled Raab's jacket, found a long bill holder full of five-hundreds of several currencies. Taking the lot, I skimmed off three for the old man, bounced back upstairs. "Is he sober enough to steer?"

After the currency disappeared into filthy trousers, he waved us aside and stepped behind the wheel. His doughy features sagged like old socks. Nodding ahead, he spoke to Stacy.

"There is a lock several miles downstream," she

translated. "He thinks we should clean up the glass, pull the pieces out of the window frames, put caulking in the outside bullet holes. There is a seam sealant in the stowage locker. Otherwise the police might be notified."

For the first time, I tucked the gun out of sight. At least until he found Cha-Cha under the towel, he seemed willing to shift loyalty to the paying customer.

"When you were downstairs," Stacy said, "he asked whether you had killed the others. I said they were all ashore except Raab. I said you probably wouldn't decide to kill anyone on this trip."

25

WE CLEANED UP THE WORST EVIDENCE OF THE SKIRMISH. I gave Stacy the automatic I had taken from Raab and went below to tear apart Mullins's cabin. The little machine pistol he'd had the night before was in a black nylon duffel bag. I tried catch levers until I thought I had the idea and went upstairs carrying the gun in its bag. We were coming into sight of the lock system, where several barges were backed up ahead of us. Along the shore a road had reappeared. I stood with one hand in the duffel, watching for the limousine.

There was a festive tourist group ashore, dining at picnic tables as a radio blared out ya-yas. Jumpy as I was, I didn't shoot anybody. We passed through the lock in forty minutes.

"I think that was Bezons," Stacy said.

All Mullins had to do was get downstream and wait. We could swing about and return to Paris. But he would have somebody covering that route. If we left the river and hired a car, Mullins wouldn't know until the barge was spotted.

Staying on the boat was folly. I'd known it from the start but wanted Uncle Hugo to believe he had plenty of time for any treachery that tempted him.

Stacy came upstairs with sandwiches. "There was a loaf of pâté that didn't smell too bad. The bread is almost fresh." She handed a sandwich to Uncle Hugo, who almost smiled before filling his mouth.

Betsy clattered up the companionway, leaned forward and unloaded a half dozen bottles of beer. She scampered up the steps. "What about *him?* Do you think it's safe?"

I imagined he had worked the river under the influence of more than Algerian beer. "Go ahead."

The *batelier* wiped his mouth on his forearm in a theatrical sweep, took the bottle Betsy offered, and emptied it in two long guzzles. The beer seemed to have an instant restorative effect. His eyes brightened, and his expression softened into mere misery.

"Ask Uncle Hugo where the next city is," I said to Stacy.

She did and reported, "Rouen is a few hours downstream."

"How large is it?"

A shrug, snorts, a waving hand. She translated: "An industrial city. We'll run into factories in the outskirts before Rouen. It could be worse, sweetheart. It's summer and we're cruising the Seine."

We came around an ambling, right-angle bend in the river, where either bank was a rising slope of farmland basking in the yellow light. Copses of willow bent close to the water. Sometimes there was a bicycle or foot path on either shore but no more road. It felt like a long way to the next town. But in twenty minutes buildings began to appear ahead, then a cluster of cramped mansard roofs. The town looked claustrophobic, compressed between the river and a forested hill. It was a big enough place to rate a Roman bridge that stretched in three pockmarked arches across the water. Uncle Hugo aimed us for the opening at mid-channel.

As we passed the town's main dock, I felt an emotional tug toward shore. We could tie up and head south. But probably not by car. The chances of finding a rental here seemed remote, and we would be more conspicuous than in a large city.

We were fifty feet from the bridge when a man leaned over the balustrade, just above a black stain crawling up one pillar, and glanced quickly upriver.

It was Habibi.

Betsy was sitting on the floral couch that Raab had occupied the previous evening. Stacy leaned against a glassless window frame, watching the town scene unfold. She was closer. I grabbed her arm. "Get below. They're on the bridge."

As I reached for Betsy the last panes of glass in the front windows exploded inward. A *pock-pock-pock* sounded on the wall behind me. Slugs ripped through wood and cushions. Uncle Hugo flung himself screaming from the wheel and wallowed across the deck.

Betsy huddled on the couch against the flimsy outer wall, head and shoulders just below the window.

I reached her just as Habibi dropped from the bridge to the barge's bow thirty feet in front of me. He landed hard, stumbled among bicycle chassis, and disappeared beneath the angle of the long deckhouse roof. In an instant he straightened and fired half a clip from his pistol. Splinters flew from the window frame.

We powered under the bridge and the light dimmed. Ducking, I put my lips close to Betsy's ear. "Lie on the deck. You'll be safe. From this angle, his shots will be high."

She slid to the floor, eyes wide. A fragment of something had opened a tiny gash on her bare shoulder. She saw the flowing blood. "Am I shot?"

"No, you're okay. Stay against the couch." For some reason we both were whispering.

"Who's shooting?"

"Habibi."

"The little creep."

As I edged away from Betsy, Stacy caught my eye from the companionway. She held Cha-Cha's pistol with one hand, the top stair with the other.

"Don't go forward," I said. "We've got a boarder. He may come through the deckhouse."

A resounding crash shook the roof, followed by a softer clatter. A second boarder. Mullins had arrived.

On my belly, I reached the wheel and gave it a hard spin. The barge responded sluggishly. We missed the stone column I had been hoping to clip and broke into daylight.

Squatting behind the wheel, I collected the duffel bag and pulled out Bruno's machine pistol. I checked the windows on my right, then straight ahead, then left, then behind me. If Mullins had any sense, he would reach a gun down through a window and spray the cabin. I craned to see out the window behind my head. There was just a sliver of sky with moving clouds. Mullins could have been a few inches out of sight yanking the pin from a grenade. Four exposed fronts couldn't be defended.

I caught Betsy's eye, nodded to the companionway and mouthed: *"Move fast!"*

She looked from me to the opening. Didn't move.

I put the gun on the deck, wormed across splinters and glass over to her. I took her arm above the elbow. Reluctantly, she brought a knee up, then the other. I nodded silently, wondering why Mullins was giving us so much time.

She moved woodenly.

She was halfway across the deck when Habibi opened up. An overhead light burst. The top of the wheel exploded. As Stacy reached up, Betsy tumbled into the companionway.

On the roof, Mullins stirred. Trying to be quiet. It was impossible to hear his direction over the slushing water and the engines' rumble. I dived for the companionway as a barrage of shots crashed through the ceiling. I went down the ladder face first, landed hard, and clung to a wall praying he wouldn't empty the clip through the deckhouse roof.

When the shooting stopped, it was almost like silence. My ears couldn't detect engine or water noises or my own breathing. I looked around. There was a tiny galley off the left side of the passage. Under a fold-down work table, Stacy crouched with an arm around her sister, gripping the automatic.

Unfortunately the machine pistol was still by the wheel.

It was the last thing I wanted to do. I turned around and crept up the steps. Stuck my head up. Wasted effort. Mullins's slugs had made hash of the gun.

I pushed away with my palms and slid down the ladder.

Stacy held out the automatic. Not much use, unless you were standing as close as Raab had been. I took it and went down the passage toward the bow.

Uncle Hugo was nowhere to be seen.

At the end of the corridor, three wooden steps led to the door onto the front deck. I stopped and tried to listen. There was a high, vaguely festive note ringing at a great distance. It could have been a call to Christmas mass, or Habibi pulling a bird's wings off, or hearing coming back to my ears.

The door opened a crack.

Habibi poked the barrel of his gun inside.

It was an unfair confrontation. He was staring into gloom. I was staring at a backlit shadow cut by a sliver of light. I aimed at the center of the shadow and pulled the trigger five times. He went backward and the door closed.

I couldn't hear even Christmas chimes.

I decided not to make his mistake and went through the door as fast as I could—at least as quickly as a man with a cane climbing a ladder could—and landed on my belly too close to Habibi. He stared at the pretty sky with a foolish grin.

No shots came from atop the pilothouse at the barge's stern. I elbowed around and waited.

Glancing forward, I was too low to see more than a few gabled roofs moving past.

Mullins, at the other end of the barge, was a good waiter. Too patient for me.

On my knees, I crouched against the slatted wall and risked a glance over the roof.

Mullins sat at a higher level, on the pilothouse roof. When my head came up, his right arm lifted. But the hand held no weapon. The arm dropped back.

There was something about his posture.

Not kneeling, not standing, not quite sitting but more sitting than anything else. There were no chairs on the roof.

I looked again.

Then I scrambled onto the deckhouse and ran through the maze of Uncle Hugo's scrapyard to the stern. From fifteen feet, Mullins's position still looked odd, almost comical. I mounted a narrow ladder to the top of the pilothouse.

He was sitting on a section of bicycle frame in the middle of a jungle of cannibalized parts. Sitting in a cruel hold. The frame was upside down, seat and handlebars on the deck, frame bars pointed upward. The metal tubing probably hadn't been sharp. But a drop of fifteen feet from the bridge had been enough to force the shaft through the trousers and into a natural opening.

I couldn't have guessed how far the section had penetrated except that the front of his khaki shirt bulged just above the belt. His knees were bent, as if he had tried to keep some of his weight off. Whether he had lost that struggle all at once or a half inch at a time didn't matter except to his dignity. In the circumstances it was remarkable that he had managed to empty even one clip into the roof. The machine pistol lay a few inches from his fingers.

His skin was greenish. His teeth were clenched. His blue eyes were vague and dreamy. Maybe he was back working at his Swiss bank. Or mixing cocktails at Baden-Baden.

The bastard couldn't have had a soul. What hissed between his teeth was just a long, bitter, frustrated sigh.

26

We motored into the stone quay a moment later.

On the grinding contact, the old wooden bow splintered. The engines chugged at the same tempo. We slid along the rough stone, breaking loose a railing. Fifty feet ahead a half-dozen barges were berthed together in a floating campground. On neighboring boats, two women who had been jabbering through their laundry lines stopped and looked upstream in horror.

I climbed down into the pilothouse and reversed the engines. The jarring progress ceased a few yards from the clotheslines.

"Are you okay?" Stacy said from the companion-way.

Uncle Hugo stumbled along the side deck, feet catching in an underbrush of bicycle parts. He clasped his forehead as he inspected the stove-in section of gunwale. At the bow, he cried out to the fellow *bateliers*, gesturing at the pilothouse. He jumped to the shore and walked aft, cursing as he surveyed the damage.

"Is it safe?" Stacy whispered.

"Yes. Mullins shot Habibi," I lied.

"What about Mullins?"

"Cycling accident."

I went down to the deck and tossed a line across. Uncle Hugo ignored the rope. Turning his back, he dodged a truck rumbling down the cobblestone road and broke into a gelatinous trot. He disappeared up a side street.

I jumped across and made the aft line secure.

The *batelier* mothers were getting an eyeful of Habibi through the shattered bow. He didn't look much like a victim of flying timbers.

A hundred yards upstream klaxon horns blared as the police converged on the bridge. The shooting had started there. The officials hadn't associated that alarm with a barge having a parking problem downstream. That would take about two minutes.

I helped Betsy ashore, put out a hand for Stacy as a small tan official car peeled off from the bridge and rocked down the street. As three provincial policemen spilled out, she gestured at the barge. *"Terroristes, messieurs!"*

The cop who sprang out nearest the barge was dark-skinned and mustached. He was tall enough to have a fair view of Mullins on the pilothouse. He drew a gun and pointed it.

Stacy explained cheerfully, *"Mort, mort.* Donald got him first."

Another vessel had passed under the bridge and was swinging toward shore. It was squat and red, with an open rear deck, making good time before a heavy wake. Astraddle the bow sat a man with a blond crew cut, khaki slacks, and an automatic rifle. A yard closer he looked more Texan than Prussian. Greg Lord came onto the deck and stood behind him.

"Do you think we can get the cops to start shooting?" I asked Stacy.

"Oh, no! Look!" Her sister raced to the edge of the water, waving furiously. On the police boat, the small suntanned shape of Charlie Kimball was running along the side deck, almost dancing.

Too late for a sensible solution, I thought. The nearest policeman showed no inclination to open fire.

Greg Lord came ashore first. "Is everything secure here? Where's Raab?"

"I cut his throat," I said. Charlie Kimball climbed off the police launch, grinning with silly relief, gloating at the sight of two safe daughters. When I got within two feet, he stretched out a hand for congratulations, or good fellowship, or something. He knew an Irish stockbroker could never keep up with a devious mind like his. I said softly, "Stuff it, you little shit."

Two pretty faces looked at me in shock.

I went over to Jock Mizel. "Your frog buddies might catch a guy named Kostelanetz if they close off the roads. There's an abandoned pier up near Bezons or somewhere. He's headed from there probably back toward Paris."

"Uh, we got that covered. Your father-in-law is a good man to know, buddy. That old boy can sure kick ass."

"He's not my father-in-law. And he gets away with it because the asses always owe him something." I felt more disgusted than angry.

"Well, he got things moving with the locals. And he stirred up the bees at the embassy. We'd have caught up with you an hour ago if we hadn't got distracted upriver."

A French officer in plain clothes came to the boat railing, hands on prim hips, and called something down.

Mizel shouted back, "Kos-te-la-netz!" He sighed. "Jesus. That's our captain from the national police. He's in charge of spin control."

When Charlie came up with two adoring daughters, I managed to be civil. He offered his hand again. "Glad everything worked out. Stacy, I'm afraid Donald still blames me for getting him involved with Greg. I'm truly sorry, Donald, for the strain you've faced."

What I blamed him for was not pulling the strings within his reach the moment the girls had left for Paris. He had been distraught, all right, but his mind had clicked along unimpaired. He had Greg's assurance of close surveillance. He had the knowledge that Raab wouldn't benefit from harming his daughters. And he had a hope of getting a better look at Raab's operation without cost. He ran the family business by seizing low-risk opportunities. Any other method of calculation would have puzzled him.

I wondered what he was getting from the Treasury in return for so much help. Didn't bother to ask. If they had him over a barrel, I might be tempted to feel sorry for him, which would be dangerous.

"Donald should have known we could count on Charlie Kimball," Stacy said.

Jock Mizel put a hand on my shoulder. "Our captain wants you to come with us and see something. Just you, McCarry." He pointed to the police boat, added softly, "Did you really cut Raab's throat?"

Hating to lose his dawning respect, I said, "He's tied up below. Don't tell Lord."

He did anyway, of course.

207

27

DMITRI KOSTELANETZ SAT IN THE BACK SEAT OF HIS BLACK Citroen. The door was open. Kostelanetz looked perturbed, as if someone had told him he had suffered a lousy day in the market. His blunt-snouted face was made for looking perturbed. The round eyes bulged in annoyance. The mouth was a scallop of disapproval. He seemed particularly indignant about the holes, one just below the right eye where the snout joined the cheek, the other diagonally higher and almost hidden in the white thicket of brow.

Jock Mizel leaned on the top of the door, kicked absently at a shard of glass. Under the cool, pale sky dozens of policemen combed the glass pebbles and other debris that littered the pier like moraine from an ice age. Fifty feet away the senior cop conferred with Greg Lord over the prostrate corpse of a man in a chauffeur's uniform. They had already shown me that one—and another. At the stale water's edge, Lord had swept a sheet back with a flourish, revealing Jerry. The torn gypsy blouse was still damp. So was the hair curling across her cheek. The concrete around her was dry except for an outline. She lay on her belly, face sideways. Her cap of wet hair hid the bullet wound.

Kostelanetz was the main attraction.

"We couldn't find any identification papers on any of them," Mizel said. "When we got here, we wasted some time looking for your bodies. Then one of the captain's people picked you up downstream."

Kostelanetz's suit coat was open, the pockets of his jacket and trousers turned out. "McCarry, are you *sure* this guy was a big shot in the organization?"

"Maybe a medium shot. But important."

"It's a pretty rough group that kills off its management because they've been exposed," Mizel said. "I'm glad we don't do that."

"Maybe you've never been exposed," I said.

He snorted. A radio squawked, and an officer approached the French captain. Mizel and I walked over to eavesdrop.

Mizel chuckled. "Paris talked to Kostelanetz's secretary. *Monsieurie Capitaine* has just learned that the chauffeur is Claude Lazzi, the son of a Socialist Cabinet minister."

The captain waved a finger at us. "Not an *important* minister. We have thirty-eight ministries, and Monsieur Lazzi's regulates commercial poultry. Still, the boy is of a good family. It is a puzzlement that he should become a driver."

"Maybe Kostelanetz did business with the father," I suggested.

He walked around the body, narrow arms folded. Calculating a police captain's pension, dividing it by a Cabinet minister's displeasure. He declared, *"Impossible!"*

He lifted his glance to Greg Lord.

The Treasury agent shook his head. "No way. Jock, why don't you give McCarry a ride back to town? We'll get this squared away."

"I'd like to stay and help," I said. "Offer input. See how cover-ups work in France."

"Get him out of here," Lord said.

I met the Kimballs for dinner at the Ritz, where Charlie had taken suites for the three of them. I was still at my Arab dive. "Greg told me about your reporter friend," Charlie said. "What a shame it couldn't have been prevented."

"If the charade had been cut short, it could have," I said.

He pretended not to understand. He wouldn't toss and turn over Lippert. "It's strange, but Greg says that Gustav Raab is demanding protection. He believes he is a candidate for assassination."

"He doesn't know Mullins is dead and has reason to be afraid of him."

"Why is that?"

"Mullins was cleaning up loose ends. Young Lazzi, the girl, Kostelanetz. But beyond that, Raab let slip that one of Mullins's functions was as an auditor. I think he must have reported to somebody other than Raab or Kostelanetz. He had seen a number of Raab's business arrangements firsthand, and my guess is he smelled something fishy. I know that this morning Gus Raab was eager either to let me go free or to shoot me rather than let Mullins interrogate me. I can guess why. If Mullins and I talked numbers, my numbers and Raab's numbers might not match."

Charlie's mouth dropped open. "Do you mean that Raab has been defrauding his clients? Do you have proof?"

"Not a trace. And I don't much care. But it's the only thing that makes sense. Imagine yourself handling the fortunes of a bunch of old-money paranoids with nasty habits. You don't even know who most of them are. How much loyalty would you feel?"

"I see." He poured a glass of good Côtes de Bourg for Stacy, frowned as Betsy's glass nudged in. She grinned.

I followed my notion. "Raab had all the opportunity he needed. Paranoids don't get monthly brokerage statements. They don't want brokers knowing who they are. So their account balance is whatever Raab says it is. You could shave five percent a year from each account. Who would know? Who would even know how to check on you?"

Charlie's face wrinkled. Despite pretenses, he appreciated treachery. "It's a nice irony—to worry about government confiscations yet trust your front man so completely."

"It wasn't complete trust, or there wouldn't have been a Bruno Mullins," I said. "Also, this explains why Raab sent one of his killers around to take care of me—why he sent Jerry after Mullins had lured your daughters over here. Your good behavior was assured. I wasn't going to get out of line. But if Mullins was suspicious of Raab Capital, he might twist my arm for information. Raab didn't want that."

"But Raab didn't try again to have you killed," Stacy said in a matter-of-fact tone worthy of Charlie.

"He was using his organization's hatchet man, or woman. He couldn't try too often. He might have to explain why. Deciding who got killed was probably Mullins's franchise. And from Mullins's vantage, I was a source of information—both about Raab and about the government's investigation."

"Worth keeping around for a while," Stacy said.

Betsy gave a smile, extending a fragile hand. "Donald is worth keeping longer than a while."

"You're cut off," her sister said. She frowned at me. Her father watched, trying to guess how things were between us. He probably wanted Stacy to be happy, however he defined happiness. He certainly didn't want me in the formula. Besides being a ne'er-do-well, I knew what a prick he was. Every frown Stacy threw me was potentially good news.

He picked up the menu card. "Well, Donald, you seem to have won over an inexperienced heart."

I patted Betsy's hand to give him something to worry about.

28

MAGEE & TEMPLE WAS A COMFORTABLE PLACE TO COME home to. Timmy Upham, having tended my accounts, had resisted investing them all in speculative two-dollar stocks. He expected thanks and got them. Thumbs behind his suspenders, lower lip thrust out, he announced that Federica was considering a reconciliation. He glanced over his shoulder. "It will be hard on Meg. But the family is the natural nucleus. Anything else is aberrant."

"Without your hotel bills, Meg won't know where to spend her money," I said.

"I'm taking the kids to Disney World. They should see what their country's like."

I looked but his face was straight. I suggested, "If you dash off an internal memo on Disney stock, you could write off the trip."

He shook his head. "That would be a bad example for the kids. They're my life."

When he left I punched Isaiah's extension. "Have the brain eaters been at work while I was gone?"

"They don't stop here anymore," Isaiah said. "Welcome back. Mad Max has a new deal for us to sell. Qwik-Lik Lube Shops," he said, spelling it out, "a limited partnership, selling commission to you and me seven and a half percent of the gross. I'm putting my mother's Hebrew teacher into it."

"A mitzvah," I said.

"It should take at least a year before it falls apart. By then, Mother's Hebrew lessons will be over."

It was great to be back.

Charlie Kimball called two afternoons later and said, "There's an item in today's *International Herald* that might interest you." He refused to read it to me. I hunted up a copy at the Chambers Street station and found the item on the inside, just a paragraph.

Munitions Executive, 52

Prince Ricard de Bora, managing director of a family-controlled Tuscany arms manufacturer, was killed yesterday in an explosion at Bora Pistola Fabriccione's main plant outside Piombino. He was 52 years old and had assumed the post of managing director two years ago after the merger of the company and an Elba mining concern controlled by the Turani family.

Not a recommendation for Raab's good health. I hoped the Frenchies and Lord took good care of him.

I went back to the office and stopped at the board room to watch the market's close. Prices hadn't done much for several days, and the ranks of hopeful losers were thin. When I got on an elevator, Magee & Temple's illustrious chairman, Thornton Wacker, got on after me. He stared sternly at the mirrored wall above the floor buttons, wasting all the perfect hair and bespoke flannel on a carload of secretaries and one indolent broker. As we passed the twelfth floor, the last secretary jumped off.

The image of patience, Thorny Wacker tucked his hands into his trouser pockets. He probably assumed I worked for him. He no more would have a name for me than for the pigeons on a window ledge. Without glancing away from his own splendid visage, he mumbled something—which I didn't catch, though it might have been a rehearsed plea that we all pull together to sell Qwik-Lik.

Then he repeated himself: "I've heard that you manage *quiet* money, Mr. McCarry."

He got off on his floor and walked away.

The chilling new tale of psychological terror by an acclaimed and brilliant mystery writer

FRANCES FYFIELD

"Frances Fyfield is remarkably thorough in her psychological profiles...she certainly understands the pathos of those people who are caught up in their dark mischief."—*The New York Times*
This is the spellbinding tale of suspicious characters and potent chemicals that will keep mystery and suspense fans turning the pages. You'll be up nights wondering if a mysterious death was really murder and if a grieving husband is really a cold blooded killer in

DEEP SLEEP

Coming In Hardcover In March 1992

POCKET BOOKS

Courtroom drama that invariably yields "crackingly dramatic scenes and some surprising turns."
—*L.A. Times Book Review*

RULES OF EVIDENCE

A NOVEL BY

JAY BRANDON

AUTHOR OF FADE THE HEAT

Delve into a world of drug dealers, informers, crooked cops, and racism and discover a first-rate reading experience that lingers long after the verdict is read and the last page is turned. You won't want to miss a word of the spine-tingling tale of courtroom suspense.

Coming in Hardcover in March 1992

POCKET
BOOKS